THE EXPLORER'S CODE

THE EXPLORER'S CODE

ALLISON K. HYMAS

[Imprint]
MAKE YOUR MARK
New York

[Imprint]
MAKE YOUR MARK

A part of Macmillan Publishing Group, LLC
120 Broadway, New York, NY 10271

Library of Congress Cataloging-in-Publication Data is available.

ISBN 978-1-250-25885-4 (hardcover) / ISBN 978-1-250-25886-1 (ebook)

Our books may be purchased in bulk for promotional, educational, or business use. Please contact your local bookseller or the Macmillan Corporate and Premium Sales Department at (800) 221-7945 ext. 5442 or by email at MacmillanSpecialMarkets@macmillan.com.

Book design by Elynn Cohen

Imprint logo designed by Amanda Spielman

First edition, 2020

1   3   5   7   9   10   8   6   4   2

mackids.com

A stolen book is a damaged map:
Seek for treasure, but it's a trap.
If you take what isn't yours,
Find disappointment behind locked doors.
Search forever, your strength exhaust,
But never find what you have lost.
Prizes will vanish, hopes fade to dust,
Should you steal, and break my trust.

*Dedicated to Chrisanne Hymas,
my curly-haired, adventurous sister.
You make everything fun.*

ANNA HENDERSON did not want to like Idle-wood Manor, but as soon as her eyes spotted the gray stone mansion emerging from the thick Virginian Shenandoah forest, her heart lifted out of her scuffed tennis shoes.

It's just some old house, Anna told herself. *Just like the ones in Mom's British TV dramas. It's probably full of vases, picture frames, and stuff I'm not allowed to touch.*

But in the gray light of a rainy morning, the house looked slightly mysterious. Like the kind that had secret passages and maybe a ghost or two.

"Oh, it's charming!" Anna's mom said as the car rattled toward the house. "So elegant."

"Serene place. Good work, Charlie!" her dad said.

Anna pushed a loose red curl behind her ear and looked over to see what her younger brother Charlie thought about the house.

1

Charlie was staring out the window, his glasses sliding down his nose. Anna couldn't be sure if he even saw the building in front of him, his sky-blue eyes were so unfocused. In his hands he clutched a piece of paper, wrinkled and worn from all the times Charlie had pulled it out to look at it.

Anna bounced in her seat, trying not to think about the way her stomach twisted when she saw that paper. She knew what it said. It was all anyone ever talked about anymore.

The car came to a halt outside the front gates of the grounds. A youngish man in jeans and a plaid button-down, with sandy hair that failed to cover ears that stuck out like satellite dishes, was waiting for them. "Hello, folks," he said after Anna's dad rolled down the window. "Welcome to Idlewood. Can I get your names?"

"We're the Hendersons," Anna's dad said.

"Ah. The contest winners." The man looked into the car and smiled at Anna. "You must be the math whiz."

Anna's mom smiled and reached back to pat her son's leg. "Actually, that would be Charlie," she said.

Charlie jolted out of whatever world he was lost in. "Huh?"

Anna looked away. She tapped her fingers on her knees. *Think about Idlewood, not how we got here.*

"Well, congratulations anyway," the young man said. "You know, I wasn't really into math when I was a kid. History was more my thing. Maybe that's why I stuck around this place . . ." He trailed off as the Hendersons stared blankly, then he took out a physical key and unlocked the gate. "Sorry, just making conversation. I'm Garrett. I'll be taking care of the grounds for the weekend. Parking is to the left of the house. It's clearly marked, so you should have no problems. Have a great weekend."

Anna's parents thanked Garrett the Gateman and drove through. As they approached Idlewood, Anna examined it. Three stories and a tower. That was a good sign. All exciting houses had a tower.

Yes. This could be a lot of fun!

"Look, honey," Anna's mom said, reaching back to wave at her daughter. "They have a pond. Maybe one of these days we could take our lunch out there and have a picnic."

Anna grinned at her mom. "Great! Or we could go swimming."

"Didn't bring our suits," her dad said. "Besides, the water is probably full of parasites."

"That's what makes it fun," Anna said. She folded her arms. "Are you sure we can't? Just for a little while?"

Her mom sighed. "I know this isn't the kind of vacation you hoped for, but at least you get a couple of days away from school."

Her dad snorted. "The school gets a couple of days away from *her*."

"David!" her mom said. She turned to her daughter. "Now, Anna, this is a very fancy house."

"I can see that." The twisting in Anna's stomach got stronger. *Here it comes.*

"Then you can also probably see what I'm getting at," her mom added. "While we're here, I want you on your best behavior. All right? None of that business with Mrs. Schwartz's attic or with the school trip to the art museum."

"The art museum wasn't my fault. I told you, I lost track of time."

"How is that related to the fact that they found you poking around a restricted area?" her mom asked, and Anna looked down.

"It wasn't *my* fault the exhibit wasn't technically open yet," Anna said. "Besides, Egyptian mummies seemed way more interesting than the Monet exhibit we were supposed to be looking at."

As for the Mrs. Schwartz thing, if she hadn't wanted Anna to poke around her attic, she shouldn't have locked the door and specifically told Anna the space was off-limits. It was practically an invitation.

Virginia Maines, the greatest explorer who ever lived, would have seen it that way.

Her father sighed. "Anna, that's not the point."

"The point," her mother said, taking over, "is that this very old house probably is full of very old, very expensive things. I want you to promise that you'll be careful and not break anything."

A hot surge of anger flooded Anna's veins. When had she ever broken anything? Sure, she'd poked around, but she had never, *ever* damaged anything that she'd found. "How reckless do you think I am?"

"Anna."

"Fine. I promise." Anna glanced at Idlewood again. This time, though, the house looked more like a prison.

Her mother nodded. "This will be fun," she said. "You should be proud that your brother won us a place here."

Right. Anna glanced at Charlie, who was still gazing at the sky. His mouth moved as he wandered his own little haven where everything was made of numbers.

Charlie, the golden child. Anna had so many memories from when they were little, running around parks and turning over rocks to see what kinds of bugs lived under them. They were only a year apart and had been each other's best friend.

But that was before the perfect math scores. Before Charlie won the Good Behavior Award year after year, and before Anna got caught climbing around on the roof of the school during recess. Before Charlie got honor roll and Anna got a special policy that required she be watched by a teacher at *all* times.

"Look, they have lawn chairs!" her mom said. "Won't that be a nice place to read when it's sunny?"

Anna shook her head. She traced a swirling pattern on her knee, then reversed it, wondering, not for the first time, if she was adopted.

Her dad worked in an office, day after day, looking at the same little walls in the same little room. Her mom stayed home with the kids, watching her British dramas and reading books in her spare time. And Charlie had turned into a clone of them, his nose in a book all the time. The gifted boy had no time for childish things like playing in the woods.

Maybe that was why Anna's parents preferred him. Charlie the math whiz, winner of weekend getaways, a year younger than her thirteen years but able to sit still for hours, reading, just like them.

Why can't you be more like your brother?

Anna, look at how quiet Charlie is being.

Charlie, keep an eye on Anna while we go out.

The last was the worst. How many older sisters had to be *watched* by their little brothers?

It would be easier to act like Charlie. Her parents would approve of her, and Charlie wouldn't look down on her anymore.

Easier but not better. She wouldn't be Anna anymore. She couldn't love school like Charlie did, the too-small box, itchy on her skin and tight on her mind. A place where everything was known, categorized, and filed away. Nowhere to explore, and no secrets to uncover. How could she be at ease sitting there when there were attics and mummy exhibits to sneak into? What was sitting at a desk and reading compared to circling the world in seventy-two days like Nellie Bly?

She'd mentioned that to Charlie once, and he'd replied that with changes in technology, she could circle the globe by plane in about thirty-six hours. Yeah, she could, she'd said, but that wasn't the *same*. Tell that to Bly. Tell it to Amelia Earhart or Osa Johnson or Jeanne Baret. Tell it to Virginia Maines. *She'd* explain that, from the ground, you could see that the world was full of shadowy corners, places still undiscovered.

At least that was true back in 1920. Anna hoped it still was, even in a world with thirty-six-hour circumnavigation.

Anna's dad parked the car beside a few others (they must not be the first guests), and Anna hopped out as soon as the engine stopped. She looked up at the house. From here, Idlewood's size was far more impressive. It didn't exactly loom, but it did seem to . . . wait, as though politely allowing its guests to judge it for themselves. Or like—what was the phrase from her mom's shows? Like it was keeping its own counsel.

The wind blew, tickling Anna's neck with her loose curl, once again unfastened from behind her ear. The air smelled like wet stone and car exhaust as another car pulled up beside them. The sick twisting in her stomach turned back into a fizzing thrill.

Such a big house. A house like this would have many rooms. Dark ones, dusty ones, not visited in many years. Maybe even an off-limits attic or a display of mummies. Sure, it wasn't an ancient tomb, but for a single weekend, maybe Anna could find a few secret places. Maybe enough to last her three days.

❖ ❖ ❖

The car door slammed, but Charlie ignored it. *Idlewood Manor*, he thought. *Rwovdllw Nzmli when translated into the Atbash cipher, and in the A1Z26 cipher it would be—*

Something pounded on Charlie's window. He

7

jumped and saw Anna outside, fist against the glass. "Hey," she called. "I don't care if you did get us here; you still need to carry your own luggage."

"Right. Sorry. I'm coming." Charlie pushed his glasses up his nose and scrambled out of the car to pick up his duffel bag. The letter from the school district was still in his hand, though wrinkled and now a bit sweaty. Before folding it and tucking it into his pocket, Charlie read the paper one more time.

"Dear Mr. Henderson," it began. (Charlie loved that in this case, *he* was "Mr. Henderson.")

> *Congratulations on winning first prize in your math competition! We are pleased to extend to you and your family a space at the exclusive Idlewood Manor open house weekend. Leave the modern world behind and spend three days living like generations past.*

After that, it was all information on how to RSVP, what to take, and what to leave at home. No pets allowed, and they were serious about the rule against modern technology. Charlie's parents were going to leave their cell phones in the car, and all Charlie had brought for entertainment were a few books, a notebook, and a pen. But Charlie still loved to hold on to the letter. It gave him a thrill to know everything that was happening was because of *him*.

After he'd won the competition, and when his teachers had told him that the grand prize was a weekend getaway at Idlewood, he'd been happy. But when he'd told his parents and his mom had smiled so much, and had told him that Idlewood hadn't been open to guests in years, he was ecstatic. Math was all well and good on its own, but when he could use it to make his parents so happy, well, that was something special, wasn't it?

But Anna had frowned while his parents celebrated, and as the family prepared to travel, she had seemed to retreat into the forest near their house more and more. And that morning, her gray eyes had been stormier than usual, and she'd glared at Charlie when he suggested that if she didn't bring any books, she could borrow one of his.

Charlie sighed. He should have known not to offer Anna a book. She wasn't the kind to sit and read. You just had to look at her behavior at school to see that. Sitting quietly, or thinking ahead, weren't favorite activities of hers.

On the other hand, Charlie couldn't seem to stop thinking, especially if it was about math, or, even better, puzzles. One of the books he'd brought was a guide to all kinds of codes and ciphers. He'd spent the drive playing around with the Atbash cipher, a simple code made by reversing the alphabet.

If A=Z and B=Y and so on and so on, then my name would be Xszoriv. And Anna's would be—

"Charlie!" Anna shouted, breaking him, once more, out of his thoughts. She was walking into the house. Into Idlewood, the mansion that he'd won a vacation at for his family. "Come on!" she said. "We're wasting time."

Charlie groaned and followed his sister. But as

startling as it was to be shaken out of his thoughts, he was glad she'd done it. Exciting things tended to happen when Anna was around. No one would ever say that about Charlie. Anna might get into a lot of trouble when she got caught in the neighbor's fenced backyard, but she was like her hair: vibrant, untamed, alive. She'd think nothing of making herself comfortable on a tree branch twenty feet off the ground (a thought that made Charlie's knees weaken even when he was safe on the ground).

Anna, the older and braver. She used to lead him on terrifying adventures in the woods, just the two of them climbing trees and jumping streams. But he always made it home safe and feeling a little bigger, a little braver, himself. Then he started school and found books (books!) and ways of going on adventures without having to risk life and limb, and so he did.

And one day he looked up and realized Anna had slipped away, preferring to play by herself than with him. Sometimes, Charlie thought, *Good riddance to your stupid, reckless adventures*, but more often he saw himself through her eyes: a bespectacled, chubby coward, dreaming heroic dreams but too scared to do anything but complete another puzzle book.

"Come on!" Anna called, and Charlie hurried up.

"I'm just taking it all in," he said.

"Oh, yeah? What shape is the doorway?" Anna asked.

Charlie thought. He hadn't noticed. "Rectangular," he said. "All doors are."

"Wrong. It's arched, like in a medieval castle," Anna said, grinning. She looked better than she had when they'd left home early that morning. The storm in her eyes seemed more lively than angry, and even her bright red hair seemed to gleam.

She's found something she likes here, Charlie thought. *Good.*

Odd, how he could completely miss the shape of the door but notice his sister's change of mood. Maybe it was the change that made it noticeable. A door was a door, but a smile had become rare.

Please like it here, Charlie thought. *We could have a good time together.*

They entered the main hall and both kids stopped, mouths open. Charlie had never seen a house like this. Dark wood panels made up the walls, and the floor was spread with a lush red-and-gold carpet. To the left was an ornate door with flowers carved all over it, with a statue of a dragon to its right. An identical dragon statue sat across the room, staring at its mate. Chandeliers tinkled overhead, and straight ahead was a grand staircase. The overall effect was like a hunting lodge meshed with a palace.

Anna grinned. "This might be great," she said.

Charlie grinned back. Anna seemed closer to him than she had for a long time. "As long as you don't break anything," he teased.

The storm returned. "I don't break things!" she said. "I'm not completely hopeless."

"I didn't say you were," Charlie said, but he wasn't able to finish.

A man came out of a side door (not the one with the carved flowers) and approached them. "Hello," he said. "I assume your parents are coming?"

Charlie saw Anna stiffen beside him, though he wasn't sure why. The man, older than Charlie's parents, wore a neat suit, gray like his hair, and he was smiling. Maybe it was because the smile was odd, held just a little too tight. *This man doesn't like kids*, he thought. That must have been what Anna saw. It was like a code. In any problem or code, once you found the thing that stuck out, like a stray thread, you could pull and easily unravel the rest. If the man's smile was unusual, there was a reason for it. It didn't take much to figure out the reason.

Charlie's parents entered the hall, carrying their own luggage. "Anna, don't run off like that!" their dad said.

"I just wanted to go inside. Isn't that what we're supposed to do?" Anna said.

The gray man approached Charlie's parents. "Welcome to Idlewood. I'm Evan Llewellyn, the owner. We're happy to have you here."

"Happy to be here," Charlie's mom said. "We're the Hendersons. You have a magnificent house."

"I rather think so," Mr. Llewellyn said. He glanced around the room, and his smile seemed to stiffen even more. He handed the Henderson parents a packet of papers. "A history of the house is in there, as well as the activities itinerary and meal menus for the weekend.

Now, I'm sure you have had a long journey and would like to see your suite."

"Yes, please," Charlie's mom said.

Mr. Llewellyn nodded. "You're in Suite Five. Upstairs, third door on the left. We have ten groups staying this weekend and only ten suites, so you shouldn't have to go too far to find yours. If you would like to explore the house, I recommend asking me for a tour. There's nothing I don't know about Idlewood, and," he added, looking straight at Anna, "many of our displays are rather breakable."

Charlie grabbed Anna's hand. "Come on."

He tugged her toward the stairs. She pulled free but kept walking with him. "What was that for?" she asked.

"I thought you were going to say something stupid," Charlie said.

Anna scowled. "I know when to keep my mouth shut, Charlie."

She walked ahead of him, counting doors, and just like that, the distance was back between them.

People are puzzles, Charlie thought. Once you found the odd thing out, you could solve them. But it seemed like no matter how hard he tried to puzzle out what had gone wrong between him and Anna, there was another layer of codes to uncover.

❖ ❖ ❖

"It's magnificent," Emily's mother said as they pulled up beside a dented sedan. Her eyes never left Idlewood Manor.

"Exquisite," Emily's father said. He was using his eyes to park the car, but as historians, both he and Emily's mother had spent hours poring over old photos of the manor, reading deeply into the writings left behind about it. He could appreciate it from memory.

Emily Shaughnessy had looked at all the old photos, too, but now she gazed up at the old house, tingling with as much excitement as if she were about to meet a movie star. Idlewood, built in 1885, turned into a hotel a mere fifty-odd years later. It hadn't lasted long as a hotel: The Great Depression closed a lot of small inns, and Idlewood was no exception. It lay vacant for years before being bought about thirty years ago by a private owner who closed everything but the main floor and rented out the ballroom for gala events, like weddings and murder mystery parties. No one had lived in Idlewood for decades—until now, for one weekend only.

The history radiated out of the house and the land around it, making Emily's twelve years feel like a blink of an eye. She hugged her book (wrapped in a brown paper bag and marked MATH) and smiled. "Hello, Idlewood."

Her dad stopped the car but made no move to leave it. Neither did Emily's mother, nor Emily herself. They sat silently for a moment, and then Emily's parents turned to her. "Are you ready?" her dad said. "Do you know what to do?"

"Dad, we've been over it a million times. It's not that hard."

"We know," her mom said. "But there was that last

time with the mansion in Northern California. After that, we can't assume . . . we just have to be careful."

Emily looked out the window. A couple of kids, a red-headed girl and a chunky boy with glasses, were entering the building. "I get it," she said. "I can stay quiet."

That time in California still haunted her parents. They'd come home pale and silent, and for weeks Emily had buzzed at dinner about a book she was reading about Nefertiti and forgotten pharaohs, anything to distract her historian parents from what had happened. She'd do what she could to prevent a repeat.

Her mom nodded. "Thank you."

"I've got it. But you know, I could help you out. No one's going to think twice about a kid exploring the house—"

"There's no need for that," her mom said. "This is *our* work, honey. We're glad you're so willing to help, but your job is to enjoy the weekend and not draw attention to us."

"Okay," Emily said, her heart deflating. But then she forced a smile on her face and let it trick her insides into expanding again. "It'll be fun," she said. She grinned. "I can't wait to see Idlewood!"

"That's what I like to hear," her father said, smiling. "Now, let's go see the house that Gardner built."

Emily carried her suitcase, plus her schoolbag, complete with her book—and a cheap yellow-and-pink Polaroid camera that she'd gotten for Christmas when she was six. She stopped outside the arched doors, falling far behind her parents, and snapped her first picture of the outside of Idlewood Manor. She tucked the picture away and closed her bag tightly before her parents could see the camera.

They might have made her leave her phone behind (they were sneaking theirs in), and they might want her to sit back and enjoy the vacation, but Emily had other plans.

Walking into the house, camera on her person, gave Emily a bit of a rush. On this one weekend, and after years of hearing her parents talk about their historical work, Emily was finally joining them in the field. Sure, they didn't know she was, but maybe dreamcrushers like the tall man who approached them would keep the adults locked into intense schedules, and they'd have to invite Emily to join them on the job.

Emily knew she could be helpful. But for now, she had to be quiet and stay hidden. Her parents greeted Mr. Llewellyn, the owner, but she stayed behind. She didn't really want him looking at her, remembering her. Her long black hair shielded her face, and she hunched her shoulders, acting younger than she was.

"And this is Emily," her mom said. "Say hello, Emily."

"'Lo," Emily mumbled, holding her bag closer.

"Hmm," her mom said. "She's not usually this shy."

"Shy kids don't bother me," Mr. Llewellyn said. He turned to Emily. "I hope you don't have any phones or cameras in that bag. We want to keep this retreat just that: a retreat from all modern inconveniences."

Well, of course. Cell phones would ruin everything for

you, wouldn't they? And what could cameras reveal that you want hidden? Though Emily really did like the idea of returning to an older time, if only for pretend. Until the day real time travel was invented, this was the closest thing.

"No," Emily said meekly. "Just my homework."

"Math," her mother said.

"Very good," Mr. Llewellyn said. "There's another math student staying here this weekend. Maybe you two could work together." He turned back to Emily's parents, his tone a little warmer. "It's very nice to meet you. You'll be in Suite Two. First door on the right. We have ten groups checked in, including you, and ten rooms. Your check-in materials are all in the packet I gave you. If you have any questions or if you'd like a tour, please see me. I'd be happy to help you in any way."

Help us? Help the house, *maybe. Protect it from careless kids breaking priceless antiques.* Mr. Llewellyn struck Emily as the kind of man who liked children fine, but only after they'd celebrated their eighteenth birthday.

Emily's parents thanked him, and they all went up to their room. As she stepped inside, Emily gasped at the beautiful walls with their painted landscape of Rome and the marble statues decorating the shelves and corners.

"We have the Rome suite," she breathed. She'd read that in the old days, the hotel had featured suites themed around different countries and cities, but she half thought Mr. Llewellyn would have ditched the theming. Was it politically correct to have one of the suites "China-themed" and another "India-themed"?

Still, like her parents said, looking at history *did* mean looking at all of it, the good and bad, and understanding it in context, and—looking at the large mural of a busy Roman market—Emily was glad that the room, at least, was the same as it had always been, as decreed by Mrs. Gardner. The previous owner of the house, before dying in South Carolina, had left provisions in her will that the house never be changed from what it was, and it looked like her orders were still being carried out.

It was one more way Idlewood was unique.

"We just need a Colosseum and this would be complete," her dad joked, sitting on a plush purple couch.

Emily tied back her hair and looked around. "Why is there a statue of Athena in here? That's Greek, not Roman."

"Probably a mistake," her mother said. "Or perhaps the statue has a history we don't know about, and this is actually Minerva, the Roman version of Athena. Though the style does look very Greek. Pity about the crack, though." She touched the statue's shoulder, where something must have broken or cut through the stone.

"I wonder." Emily pulled the Idlewood history page out of the packet, skimmed it, and laughed. "Very basic. Not very helpful in identifying our marble friend." She sat on the bed. "Either way, I like it here."

"Emmy, your room is that way," her dad said.

"Maybe you can get to work on that math homework," her mom said as Emily went to find her bedroom.

She found her own bed tucked in a small room

painted sky blue and marble white. It was rather pretty, but she wasn't here to take in the sights. She set her bag on the bed and took out her book and camera.

She opened the book, but instead of pages full of math problems, images of Idlewood filled each page. It was a somewhat more detailed history of the house, brand-new, self-published, from Jerry and Flora Shaughnessy, Emily's parents. Her parents' research was detailed and sound. But even the best historians' work meant nothing if it didn't impact the present world. What had happened in Northern California was proof of that.

Emily pulled a folded packet of papers from the crease, smiled at it, and then returned it to the book. Her parents would *freak* if they knew she'd brought that with her! But it was necessary. It was important evidence about Idlewood's past. Besides, it wasn't like she'd brought the *original*. It was an expendable photocopy.

She turned the page, hiding the papers, to a picture of the Gardner family, Elaine and Everett and their three kids. "Don't worry," Emily said to Elaine's smiling face. "I won't fail."

Grinning, she closed the book and scooped up the camera. With only three days to work, there was no time like the present. She would show her parents what she could do.

2

SUITE FIVE was more interesting than Anna had expected. She thought it would be some bland, beige space with weird watercolors that looked like the ocean. She was amazed and pleased to step into a beautifully decorated central room with lovely porcelain vases, interspersed with brass statues of dragons. The walls were decorated with ink paintings of mountain ranges that looked authentic, at least to Anna's limited knowledge.

A framed postcard, yellowed on the edges, read, "Greetings from Beijing." The room was clearly themed to Chinese art and architecture, and there were books about China's history, landscape, and culture on the shelf. Her parents and brother would like that.

Anna smiled, feeling, at least vaguely, the fizz of exploration. This room was *cool*, and she wanted to see every part of it.

"Can I have this bedroom?" Charlie called from down the hall.

"Sure," their mom called back. "We have three bedrooms, so you can each have your own."

Wow! Her own bedroom in a hotel? That was also cool.

Anna walked to Charlie's bedroom. It had similar colors as the main room, green and gold, though instead of the painted mountains, the walls were decorated with dragon-printed wallpaper. Whoever decorated this house must have really liked dragons. And on the wall over the bed's headboard hung a naked sword.

"Awesome!" Anna said, approaching the sword.

"I know!" Charlie was beaming. "Isn't this the greatest house you've ever seen?"

Anna nodded, touching the cool metal of the sword. On a whim, she ran a finger along the edge.

"Don't!" Charlie pulled her arm away.

Anna raised her finger. "Blunt," she said. She'd guessed it as soon as she saw the blade wasn't sheathed. Mr. Llewellyn wouldn't want anyone cutting themselves by accident. But its bluntness made the sword less interesting. The fun was in the danger, right? Otherwise, it was just a metal stick.

"I wonder what my bedroom is like," Anna said.

"Let's go see it," Charlie responded. He dumped his bags on his bed and hurried into the hall.

Anna followed him to a bedroom across from the bathroom. What kind of weapon would be hanging in her room? Another sword? Or what if her room didn't have weapons, but maybe something cooler? A huge statue of a dragon, like the ones in the entry hall, or maybe—

A painting.

Over the bed hung an intricate ink painting, with Chinese calligraphy along the edge. It was beautiful, and Anna admired the graceful lines of the painting (which was of some kind of tree), but still.

Charlie got a sword.

"What's your room like, Anna?" her mom said, appearing behind her. "Oh, that's beautiful."

It was. It really was. Anna liked it, but why did Charlie get the sword? Just because he was a boy? He wouldn't appreciate it like she would!

"Do you think Charlie and I could switch rooms?" Anna asked.

"Honey, what's wrong with this one?" As Anna tried to put her thoughts into words, her mom said, "The walls are so interesting here. Don't you think?"

"I guess." Along the walls, Anna's room had sets of wood panels painted with bamboo forests hanging all around, in columns of three. In the shadows of one picture, Anna could see a dark shape of some creature lurking.

A sinking feeling that had nothing to do with the room tugged at Anna's chest. She knew it well—it was the loss of mystery. Now that she'd seen the room, the whole suite—okay, it was gorgeous, and Anna would love to stay here. But this was a question already answered, with nothing left to discover, and Anna wasn't through discovering.

Good thing there were plenty of other rooms to explore. Maybe they were all themed. Anna dropped her bags. "Can I go look around the house?"

"Sure, but be careful and be respectful of the other guests—" her mom started, but Anna was already gone.

She began on the first floor, skirting around the entry hall where stiff Mr. Llewellyn was greeting another guest, a golden-blond man with pinkish skin in a T-shirt and blazer, with a rolling suitcase absolutely *covered* with buttons and pins, the kind you buy as souvenirs. From the moment she'd met Mr. Llewellyn's eyes, she recognized his type: He was just like all the other teachers and babysitters who wanted children to be decorative statues instead of human beings. Not exactly the best person to encounter on an adventure. So she slipped behind him as she went downstairs. The blond man raised his eyebrows at her but didn't say anything.

The first floor was the main living area and the common rooms of the house. The entry hall, with its darkly opulent look, was only the beginning. Anna found a dining room with blue walls and gold decorations and knew instantly that her mother would ooh over its elegance. It had a huge window that overlooked the grounds, and Anna spent some time admiring the expansive landscape before moving on. She'd have to spend some serious time outside, once the inside of Idlewood had been explored.

Beyond the dining room lay a parlor with a completely different color scheme of rose and lavender, and beyond that was a library. Charlie was going to go missing one of these days, and they were going to find him holed up in there. He was welcome to it; Anna would find better places to be.

In each of the rooms she looked into, Anna couldn't help but admire the interesting little touches. A ballroom held a fireplace large enough to park a car in as well as a gallery of paintings. Another room had live tropical plants and trees growing out of the floor, and Anna swiped an orange before looking for the next room.

This house is amazing! she thought, nibbling at a segment. *Who has a house with an indoor greenhouse?*

The next room turned out to be the kitchen, and a sharp-nosed, iron-haired woman in a dusty apron spotted Anna and threw a dish towel at her. "Out! No children allowed!"

That was fine. The kitchen was the last room on the first floor, but there was a whole second floor to explore.

Anna snuck past Mr. Llewellyn again. This time, he was welcoming a stately Polynesian woman with a very thick, long dark braid shot through with gray who was wearing slacks and carrying a tote bag stuffed to the brim with books. As Anna passed, the woman shifted and a book fell out. It was titled *Quantum Goldfish, Chocolate*

Dynasties, and Other Secrets. Anna couldn't even *begin* to imagine what that book would be about!

Upstairs, the first thing Anna did was walk the whole length of the hall. It was a long one; if each suite was like her family's, then they took up a lot of space. She had to walk for a while to reach each new door.

Ten doors, just as Mr. Llewellyn had said. Five on each side of the hall, odd numbers on one side, even on the other. Anna turned the corner to find a hall of sealed doors (she tried every one), which ended with a dusty bookcase littered with old, yellowed books and one cheap plastic plant. She turned around to explore the suites, since that seemed to be the most interesting thing up here.

Her family's suite was on the left, as seen from the staircase, so she started on the left side. The first suite's door was open, and a white woman was bustling around.

Anna knocked on the open door, and the woman looked up. "Sorry," Anna said. "I was just wondering if I could see your room."

"Oh, yes," the woman said. "Come in." She was a soft-looking woman, unlike the cook, and her mousy brown hair was mixed with gray strands.

Anna stepped into a frozen wonderland. The walls were white with silver snowflakes, and the sitting room furniture was in all shades of blue, from cool ice to deep midnight. The woman smiled at Anna as the girl gaped.

"Mr. Llewellyn called this the Arctic Circle suite," the woman said. "And you haven't seen my favorite part." She pointed up, and Anna followed her finger to the ceiling, which was painted with the northern lights.

"Amazing."

"Isn't it? Apparently all the suites in this house are themed like this. What's yours? I'm Rosie, by the way."

"Anna. Ours is China."

"Anna. That's a nice name. Is it short for anything?"

Anna sighed. "Annabella. It's a family name." Her great-grandmother on her father's side. Her parents were big on family names; Charlie's was also plucked from the family tree.

Rosie beckoned Anna to follow her. "While you're here, you may as well get the tour. Just not that room." She pointed at a closed door. "My husband is taking a nap. So, China. Sounds pretty."

"It is," Anna said, floored for the moment by another room with a stuffed penguin in the corner. "Was that once alive?"

"I'm not sure," Rosie said. "I wonder what the other suites look like."

"I'm exploring them," Anna said. "You could come, if you want." An adult in tow would open doors, figuratively and literally, for Anna. Besides, Rosie seemed nice.

The woman sighed. "I'd love to, but I know my Xavier would want to come, too. I'll just have to hope that the other guests are willing to give tours this afternoon. Let me know if you see anything interesting, though, okay?"

"Okay." Anna left and went to the next suite. The

guests in this one were a young black couple, who, from the sickening way they looked at each other, must have been on their honeymoon. They let Anna in to see that their suite was decorated with shells and tiki statues, and the king bed had a canopy of grass. Pacific Islands, maybe? The way the walls were painted, it seemed like the effect was meant to make the guests feel like they were staying in a tropical tree house. But Anna didn't stay long. The guests let her have the run of the room, but they kept giggling and flirting with each other, so she took a quick look around and left before she threw up.

Many of the ten suites weren't occupied yet, so Anna looked at those next. There were rooms for the Serengeti, Egypt, and India, all painted and decorated differently. Another suite, apparently Australia, judging by the didgeridoo in the corner and emu feather decorations, had a friendly family from Tennessee with young children, who all (six of them, including parents) had the same blue eyes and wore matching homemade T-shirts that read IDLE IN IDLEWOOD. They let Anna take a look around as long as she didn't disturb the youngest, who was taking a nap in the largest bedroom (make that seven). Anna agreed, but did sneak a peek through the crack of the door. She didn't see much, but it was better than nothing.

Another suite seemed to be the Amazon. Anna knocked and tried to enter, thinking it was empty, but the woman with all the books was in there, so she had to leave. She'd ask for a tour later.

But just when Anna thought each suite corresponded to a place in the world, she opened another door to reveal a room that looked like the inside of an airplane.

"Huh." Anna stepped inside. A suitcase lay on the bed, so this room wasn't empty, but when she called out, no one answered.

Someone was staying there. She shouldn't go inside without permission. But this room was so different! Anna ached to explore it. Still, maybe she should wait.

Anna shook her head. Nothing ventured, nothing gained. Virginia Maines, greatest explorer of the early twentieth century (as far as Anna was concerned), wouldn't have hesitated. When a group of men tried to stop her from traveling to Africa alone because she was a woman, Virginia walked out of the room and onto a ship to the Ivory Coast, stopping only once to buy a sandwich. If she could do that, Anna could explore a room. If she was quick, no one would know she'd ever been there.

While each of the rooms in this suite had an aviation theme (one room had a propeller over the bed), only that first entry room looked like it belonged inside an airplane. The walls were painted gray and lined with rivets, and there was even a door painted on one wall. The sparse furniture looked like chairs ripped from an old-fashioned airplane.

But the trim along the baseboard was red and intricate. Anna knelt to examine it: dragons, flying past each other. Interesting that the airplane room had a dragon motif, considering that Virginia Maines's airplane was called the—

"What are you doing here?" a sharp voice asked. Anna sprang up and spun around.

Mr. Llewellyn was at the door, with an elderly white couple in tow. The stiff house owner looked like he'd shatter into a million pieces if you tapped him. "This is not your room," he said, striding across the room and grabbing Anna by the shoulder. "You can't just walk into people's private spaces."

"I just wanted to see the room!" Anna said. "Was that so bad?"

"Oh, Mr. Llewellyn, no need to be so harsh. We all want to see all the rooms here," the elderly woman said, giving Anna a sweet smile. A huge quilted bag hung from her shoulder.

"And you will in due time, *with permission*," Mr. Llewellyn said. The elderly man nodded at his words, making his huge mustache bounce.

"I'm very sorry for this intrusion, Mr. and Mrs. Haskell. It won't happen again," Mr. Llewellyn added, glancing at his guests.

"I hope not," the man with the mustache said. "There's a right and wrong way to do things, young lady. Best to learn that now."

Anna frowned as Mr. Llewellyn pulled her into the hall. She would have asked to see the room if anyone had been home.

"Now, listen," Mr. Llewellyn said. "This house is very old. It's not like your home, where you can run around as you please."

"I know it's not the same," Anna protested. Other guests, including Rosie and Matching Shirts family and the lady from the Amazon room, were peering out to see what the commotion was. The honeymooners didn't seem to care. "I just wanted to see everything. Isn't that why people used to come for tours?"

"Yes, they used to do so, but—" Mr. Llewellyn seemed flustered. But then he straightened his gray tie and his gray face and said, "This is not a house to play in. These rooms are private now, do you understand?"

"What are they?" Anna asked. "I saw some of them. Are they all themed around places? Why?"

A snort came from behind her. Anna looked and saw a girl with long black hair and a snooty expression. Anna glared.

"When this house became a hotel, Elaine Gardner wanted each room to feel like a journey to another land," the girl said. "She designed the decorations herself, which is why they seem so . . . old-fashioned."

"Elaine Gardner?" Anna asked.

The girl smirked. "The woman who used to own this house. Didn't you learn anything about this place before you came?"

"Emily!" The girl's mother yanked her daughter aside just as Mr. Llewellyn, fed up with the bickering, led Anna away to her family, who, like the others, had come out to see what was wrong.

"I'm very sorry about this," Anna's father said, taking Anna's shoulder. "Anna is a bit of a free spirit."

"Then I suggest she be free outside," Mr. Llewellyn said. "No poking around other people's things."

Anna's face burned. "I wasn't doing that!"

But Mr. Llewellyn had gone. Stuck-up, stiff, obnoxious—Anna shook her dad off and saw Charlie standing in the door, a piece of paper in his hand.

"So you were just going to wait to do something stupid, huh?" he said.

First that Emily girl, now Charlie? Anna pressed her lips together, stood up straight, and spun on her heel.

"What are you doing?" her mom asked.

"As I'm told," she said. "I'm going outside."

Fists clenched, Anna strode downstairs, through the entry hall, and out onto the grounds and into the forest, not even stopping for a sandwich.

❖ ❖ ❖

Nice going, Charlie. He set down the page he'd been reading about the history of Idlewood and slumped against the wall.

Anna had looked so upset when Mr. Llewellyn brought her back, and what did he do? Razz her a little. She was his sister, and that was what siblings did, but Charlie had misread the situation. Again.

But no more. This vacation was a chance to start fresh with Anna. He should go apologize to her.

Although, who knew how she'd respond? What if she silently stomped off? Or screamed at him? What would hurt more, silence or rage? Maybe it was better to wait until she cooled down before he tried.

Oh, come on, Charlie! That was the fear talking! Anna was his sister, not some threatening monster. And even if it was scary, Charlie would never show her he was more than just some bookworm if he never took even a small risk like this.

That settled it. "I'm going to find Anna," he announced to his parents, who were circling items on the weekend itinerary.

His mom looked relieved. "Tell her we're not mad," she said. "But we would like to talk to her when she's ready to come in."

Charlie nodded and left the suite, closing the door behind him. Idlewood really was a nice house. Even the doors were fancy, shiny dark wood with gold numbers nailed on each one.

Charlie looked at the number 5 nailed on the door just above his eye level. *Wait a minute.* He leaned in, reaching up to touch the wood, which was slightly darker, as though it had once been protected from fading under the light—under a different metal number. The darker wood was in the shape of a number 1.

That was odd. Why had their door once been numbered "1" if it was in the middle of the hall?

Moving slowly, he walked toward the stairs, passing another suite door. Under the number 3, the dark outline of a faded number 5. Counting up? Skipping at least one number? Gears started turning in Charlie's head, but he forced them to stop. Surely there was a reasonable explanation for out-of-order numbers. No use getting involved in a code that didn't exist.

But when Charlie checked the next two doors at the end of the hall, his heart began racing and he ran downstairs, flying feet powered by the energy only the thrill of a new puzzle could give him.

The number 3 on one side, but on the other, the number 1. Odd numbers on *both* sides of the hall, and a repeat at that! The numbering on the doors didn't make sense, no matter which way you looked at it. And *that* was a problem begging to be solved.

Just wait until he told Anna!

3

EVEN THE FOREST didn't seem large enough to contain the crackling, angry energy that poured through Anna. It turned out that Idlewood really was going to be another boring, don't-touch-anything kind of place, even with its themed suites and indoor garden of tropical fruits.

She kicked at a tree, scuffing the dirt in an aimless furrow. She aimed her next kick at a mound of moss, reveling in the feel of dirt against her shoe. Yes, she knew she shouldn't have been in that room, not when other guests had claimed it. No, she wouldn't have wanted to find some stranger poking around her room without her permission, possibly stealing from her. But it wasn't like she was trying to hurt anything! She just wanted to see what the room looked like.

She kicked at a raised tree root, all covered with grass. Her foot collided with the root, tearing the grass and revealing a stick about as big as a half-used pencil wedged into the mud beside the root. But . . . wait. It looked like it had a growth or knot on it, but what knot was so perfectly round and flat? Dropping to her knees, Anna touched the stick. *It's not wood.* Quickly, she found a twig and loosened the mud around the object, which was lying almost flat against the ground. It wasn't long before she was able to pry it free.

She looked at the chunk of twisted black metal in her hand. An old nail?

No. It wasn't a nail. It was so much better. Anna stared at the old key in her hand. It looked like something out of a story, with a long shaft and two prongs on the end. What was it doing there?

The ground was at a slight angle. It rained a lot in Virginia, so perhaps the key had been dropped once, and the rain had carried it here. But that could mean it belonged to Idlewood!

Walking back to the house, Anna examined the key again. It was black, but not inherently; that came from a tarnish that covered the silver metal beneath. Its head— the flat, round part that had attracted Anna's attention— had an ornate design on it that looked like a palm tree. Did that mean it belonged in the Pacific Islands suite? She hadn't seen any locked cupboards or dressers there, or at least none with keyholes. She would have remembered a keyhole big enough for this key. Old locks were especially inviting.

What could it belong to? As Anna entered the

grounds, she considered telling Mr. Llewellyn what she'd found. It was his house, and he might know what this key would unlock. Besides, it might make a nice peace offering, after irritating him earlier.

Yeah, no. He'd probably think she stole it. Besides, Anna didn't want to be *told* what the key opened. It was better if you found it yourself.

A gaggle of elderly ladies, of different races and heights but all seeming to favor pastel-colored clothing and coconut-scented lotion, was entering the house, and behind them, another car pulled up the driveway and a Japanese couple in their thirties got out, dressed in cargo shorts, T-shirts, and stylish sport sunglasses, ready for vacation. One of them carried a bundle of cloth in her arms. When she saw Anna, she cradled the bundle out of sight and hurried into Idlewood.

Anna shook her head and peered up at the house, anger returning. Thanks to finding the key, she hadn't been out in the woods long enough to cool down. So, stupid key. Stupid Charlie and his stupid vacation prize, stupid Mr. Llewellyn throwing her out just as things were getting interesting, stupid Idlewood with its weird . . . everything.

Yes, Anna thought. Something about this house was very weird, and it wasn't just the guests sneaking who knew what in bundles of cloth into the house. Everything was just a little bit off: the indoor plants growing from the ground, the themed suites, the actual once-living penguin, and now this key. As Anna looked at it, even the outside of the house seemed wrong, though she couldn't figure out exactly what was gleaming in the shadowy corners of her brain.

And first, she needed a place to wait while her anger dissipated. Anna turned a corner and gazed up at the house's tower. There was a small ledge, just big enough to sit on, about ten feet off the ground. She ran her hand over the stones: old, chipped, jutting. Perfect. If Mr. Llewellyn wanted to complain, he'd have to find her first.

If only she could really disappear, just like Virginia Maines had. Anna loved stories about all explorers, but Virginia had risen to the top for her. She wasn't an explorer many people remembered—Anna had first learned about her in a footnote. Virginia Maines, born in Richmond in 1896, was not the first American to explore outside her country. She wasn't trying to "find the source of the Nile" or have a species of plant named after herself. In fact, she didn't care about laying claim to anything, and no zoological or geological society could claim *her* or her findings. She was a well-read banker's daughter turned adventurer, and as far as anyone knew, she just explored because she wanted to learn more about the world around her.

But Anna felt so drawn to her. Sure, they were both from Virginia, which was why she had first heard of the explorer and started reading her stories. But as she read, she found a woman traveling not for work or science but just because she could. That sheer spunk had led Virginia to circle the world dozens of times in her plane, accompanied by only a few people, but mostly her copilot David Bradley. Who knew what she could have done if it wasn't for the intriguing and frustrating way her story ended?

Anna had read all about it on the one fan site she could find about Virginia Maines. Virginia had made a name for herself in the 1920s, traveling all over the world and discovering rare artifacts, like a real Indiana Jones. Even better, she'd always handed those artifacts over to the countries she found them in. She never kept them for herself. At a time when so many explorers took what they found, Virginia was no thief.

But sometimes she was given treasures to take home. Gifts. Virginia was becoming a star, but then, one day in 1925, she vanished. She hadn't even been on a new expedition, like Amelia Earhart, or murdered in the desert, like Alexandrine Tinné. One night she was sleeping in her bed, but the next, she was gone. There was no sign of foul play, but none of her things were missing, and no trace of her was ever discovered. No one ever found her reputed stash of treasures, either. And so the world wondered, and so the world forgot.

No, Anna thought, shaking her head. That was too much. She didn't really want to disappear forever like Virginia, or be forgotten. She could settle, though, for going missing for a much shorter time by climbing out of reach.

Anna tucked the key into her pocket, then climbed, carefully choosing the most prominent stones as handholds. They were perfect; one even curled in to allow a better grip, as she discovered when her fingers landed in a small pool of rainwater. Once she pulled herself up, she found places for her feet and hands far more easily than she expected. It was like the wall was made to be climbed. She perched on the ledge, thinking, *If any adult finds me up here, that's what I'll tell them.*

Right. Like they'd listen to anything *she* had to say.

After the morning's rain, the sky had broken to reveal the sun through white, fluffy clouds. The air was warm and humid but clean-feeling and honeysuckle-scented. And, even from ten feet up, Anna felt like she could see everything.

Including her brother. "Hey, Anna!" It was Charlie, stomping across the lawn with the grace of an elephant with a twisted ankle. "What are you doing up there?"

"Sitting. That's still allowed, right? Not too stupid for you?" The anger hadn't quite died down yet, fed a little by Anna's frustration over the little . . . something . . . that wasn't adding up in her head. What was wrong with this house?

Charlie jogged over and shielded his eyes from the sun. "No. I mean, maybe, but . . . you know what you're doing, right? Sure you do."

As Anna listened, confused by his babble, Charlie added, a little out of breath, "I just wanted to apologize. I didn't mean to be a jerk back there. I'm sorry."

The anger flowed away. Charlie wasn't a bad brother. He just didn't seem to *get it*. But maybe that wasn't his fault. "It's okay," she said. "It's what siblings do, right?"

"Right." Charlie smiled and then glanced up again at the house. He pushed his glasses up his nose and gave Idlewood a sharp, focused stare. Anna recognized it—he wore the same expression when he solved his cryptograms and crossword puzzles over his Chex at home.

"What's up?" she asked. "Other than me."

Charlie laughed. "It's just that this house seems really weird."

"Tell me about it."

Charlie shrugged. "I guess all old houses would be weird to you."

That stung. Wouldn't old houses be weird to anyone? "I meant tell me about it." Anna patted the ledge beside her. "There's room for one more."

Charlie's face turned the color of the clouds overhead. "Up . . . up there?"

"Sure. It's not too hard. The stones make great handholds. Put your hand on that one right there, with the triangular part sticking out. You'll be up here before you know it."

For a moment Charlie stared at the stone and Anna stared at Charlie. *Come on*, she thought. *Come up here! Do something a little risky. Remember how much fun we used to have?*

But Charlie stepped back. "Maybe another time," he said. "I think I'm going to go back inside and explore the house a little more. Maybe see the other suites? They were cool, right?"

"Right," Anna said, slumping back. Her limbs felt heavy with disappointment, though she wasn't sure why, exactly. Charlie lived in his head, and Anna lived just beyond the reach of her hands. That was just the way things were these days.

But imagine if one day Charlie did put down his book and looked around! She'd have so many things to show him.

"See ya," Charlie said, and ran off.

Oh, right, he knew something weird about the house! "Wait!" Anna called, but Charlie was already gone.

She sighed, pushed her hair back, and considered the drop down to the ground. Could she jump, or would it be better to climb down? Better climb. Nothing worse on the first day of a vacation than a broken bone—Anna knew this from experience. (That had been an unpleasant trip to Florida, but in her defense, the pier hadn't looked rotten.)

This house seems really weird, Charlie had said. Exactly what Anna was thinking! What had he noticed? Was it the same thing as whatever was bugging her, tickling the back of her mind? Too bad he ran off before she could ask.

And now Charlie was going to go explore the other suites, like she had. But because it was Charlie, the contest winner, he'd probably get a tour from Mr. Llewellyn himself. As she thumped down into the grass, Anna could see it: the gray old man escorting Charlie and that dark-haired brat from room to room, taking them through the ballroom, letting them pick pineapples in the indoor garden. Her parents could accompany them, regaling every guest with the story of Charlie's victory and not saying a word about their inadequate daughter. Anna looked up at the house's rows of windows. Mr. Llewellyn would probably take them to the third-floor rooms and into the tower, too.

Wait. Anna looked up again, counting windows. First floor, second floor, third floor, tower. She'd seen all of them when they'd driven into Idlewood. Three floors.

So why, in all of her exploring, had she never seen a staircase or door leading to the third floor?

That was it! An adult might say that the third floor was storage, or off-limits because it was where the workers stayed. But if that were true, then there'd be a sign in front of a staircase, warning people away. That was what Anna had seen before.

Anna touched the weight in her jeans where the blackened key lay in her pocket and grinned. An old, mysterious floor of an old, mysterious house? One no one knew about? Now *that* was real exploration, the kind Virginia Maines would jump at.

And so would Anna. She dashed back into the mansion, the key bumping against her leg with every stride.

❖ ❖ ❖

The redheaded trespasser almost knocked Emily over as she raced up the main staircase. Emily had been admiring the molding, tapping a finger on the bag at her hip, when the girl had flown by, catching Emily's shoulder and spinning her around.

"Watch where you're going!" Emily called, but if the girl heard her, she didn't respond.

So Emily was left to shake her head. Kids like that were the reason adults had issues trusting kids like *her*. Emily wouldn't be surprised if before the weekend was over, the redhead ended up smashing some precious antique from the Civil War era.

Speaking of which, Emily had a job to do. Her parents were on the second floor taking pictures, so Emily tiptoed downstairs. She stopped, once, in the entry hall. *No, not here.* This was too open, too obvious. She'd have to come back later. There were plenty of other rooms to start in.

Emily tried the carved door beside the dragon statue. Locked. Okay, maybe not that room. How about the next one?

This one opened onto a classy parlor. Emily smiled. This would work great. She opened her bag, pulled out the childish camera, and snapped a picture of the wallpaper.

Emily gave the instant photo a shake as she glanced around for her next target. Maybe the furniture next? It looked old enough to potentially hide a story. She took a picture of it, as well as a few more of the walls and the room as a whole, before moving on.

There were some interesting rooms, for sure. Emily peeked into the dining room but had to leave because an older couple was sitting and enjoying the view. She lingered a while in the greenhouse, with its tropical plants. Everett Gardner had been just that: a gardener. Here was the proof of his horticultural hobbies.

She took a picture of the towering banana plants and shook her head. It was a pity, really, how little time she and her parents had at Idlewood. Which just meant Emily had to work harder.

Every detail needed to be captured. Her parents were busy finding their own evidence that Idlewood was historically more than just an old house. Emily was sure they'd get what they came for. Her parents were brilliant at uncovering history from hints and scraps.

But it was possible that those hints and scraps wouldn't be enough, and Northern California would happen all over again. So Emily had to take measures herself, especially if her parents missed or overlooked important historical evidence.

Emily left the greenhouse and heard footsteps in the hallway. She froze, then stashed the camera in her bag as Mr. Llewellyn came down the hall.

He stopped when he saw her, then approached.

"What are you doing down here?"

"I'm sorry. Aren't I allowed to be here?" Emily asked quietly, remembering her role as the shy, mousy daughter. Nothing to see here, sir. Move along.

Mr. Llewellyn smiled stiffly. "This is the public area, so yes, you may be here. I'm just surprised to find you alone."

"It was this or homework, and I heard so much about this place, I wanted to see it for myself."

"In that case, I'll show you around," Mr. Llewellyn said. "Perhaps your parents would like to join us."

No, no, no! If Mr. Llewellyn was here, Emily and her parents wouldn't be able to take their pictures! But what could she say? "Don't you have to greet guests?"

"The guests have already arrived and checked in. I have some free time now."

Fine. There would be time later to get her pictures. "Okay. My parents are resting, though, so it's just me."

Emily followed Mr. Llewellyn as he showed her the library and the parlor again, trying to act interested but not too interested. A normal kid wouldn't care about why the Gardners chose which antiques to display, or how slightly the building was altered when it became a hotel. But when he showed her the ballroom with its gallery of paintings, Emily couldn't fake indifference anymore. "Amazing!"

"You think so?" Mr. Llewellyn sounded pleased. "It is quite stunning. I think the Gardners wanted their guests to feel a little overwhelmed when they came in here."

Emily took in the grand ivory-colored walls, hung with vibrant paintings of people in silk robes. She pointed at one of a couple. "That's them, right?"

Of course it was. But Mr. Llewellyn wouldn't expect Emily to know that.

"Yes," Mr. Llewellyn said.

"How did you end up getting Idlewood?"

"Inheritance," Mr. Llewellyn said, but the smile was gone from his voice. "My father bought the house, and now it comes to me."

"It's beautiful," Emily said. Her fingers itched to take pictures, but that would have to wait. So, instead, she decided to pry a little. "It's really interesting that Mrs. Gardner insisted that the house stay exactly the same. Looking around here is like looking back in time."

Mr. Llewellyn shrugged, staring up at the painting. "Almost. Some changes have been made over the years. Modern conveniences and technology, especially in the kitchen, and I made some alterations when I cleaned this place up."

Alterations? "You changed it?" Emily asked. "Why? I thought it was supposed to stay the same, always."

Mr. Llewellyn faced Emily, smiling. "Nothing drastic. I was only correcting some errors made by past building crews. But the important things, decorations included, are all as Mrs. Gardner wanted."

Okay. That was good. Which led to Emily's big question, which was one an innocent kid could easily ask. So she did. "Why did Mrs. Gardner want Idlewood to stay the same?"

Emily watched Mr. Llewellyn carefully as he answered. He shrugged and raised his hands. "We can speculate," he said, "but I don't know. Perhaps she was attached to the place as it was and didn't want those memories to fade." He ran a hand along an armchair beside them. "Personally, I think she always intended to buy the house back, once the family overcame the Depression, but she died before she could."

That was true. Elaine Gardner had died fairly young, in the early 1940s. Her children lived with their father until they left to start their own lives, after which Mr. Gardner died after running afoul of a mountain lion while on a fishing trip. But that wasn't the story Emily wanted to hear. "Huh," she said. "After the scandal, I would have thought she'd prefer to leave those memories behind."

"The scandal." Mr. Llewellyn frowned. "You've done your reading."

Not good. Emily dipped her head and scuffed a foot along the floor. "A little. When my parents got the reservation, I searched Idlewood online. There was something in 1925 that the family never spoke about, so I figured there was a scandal."

Oh, Emily knew a lot more than that. But this was to figure out what *Mr. Llewellyn* knew.

"Yes, well." Mr. Llewellyn fixed his old, gray eyes on Emily's. "There may have been. But the past is so beautiful. It doesn't do to dwell on the ugly parts. Let's celebrate the good. Like this painting. It truly is lovely." He faced the portrait again.

The owner seemed to be aching to change the topic, which was perfect for Emily. He was uncomfortable. She could use that.

"Yes," she said. "And everything is *so* authentic. I can't imagine why anyone would want to sell this place."

Mr. Llewellyn twitched. He gave a smile that didn't quite meet his eyes (he seemed to have a lot of those, in many flavors) and looked at Emily. "Sell it?" he asked.

Play it cool, Emily. "Sure," she said. "Like how your family got it. Someone sold it, right? And someday you'll sell it."

Mr. Llewellyn's eyes widened. Emily kept her composure, holding her face in an innocent expression, watching his every move. He ran a finger along his tie.

"Maybe even soon," Emily added. "After all, it can't be easy to maintain a place like this, hidden up in the mountains away from most visitors. It's an old house. But the land is pretty. An owner could make a lot of money on a good sale, and it's not like the buyer has any obligation to keep the building as it is. But with the scandal and everything, perhaps it's best if some ugly parts of the past are covered up for good. Oh, I'm sorry. I was rambling."

"Yes," Mr. Llewellyn said. He coughed and peered at her. "How . . . ?" He swallowed, then said, "Those are some good points, and *someday* a buyer might make some similar ones. But that's a long way off."

But Mr. Llewellyn dropped his gaze and scratched his jaw, looking every inch a liar.

"So, you're not planning to sell the house, say, after this one last weekend?"

Mr. Llewellyn stiffened like she'd hit him. *Bingo.*

The big door to the ballroom opened, and another guest dragging a little rolling suitcase (the souvenir pins all over it clinked as it bumped along) and a nice-looking couple peered inside. "Hello?" the woman called. "Mr. Llewellyn, are you in here? There's a man named Garrett who says he has a call for you."

"What? Yes, yes. I'm coming." Mr. Llewellyn threw another glance at Emily and hurried out of the room.

Both men followed him, but the woman frowned at Emily. "He seems a little rattled. What happened?"

"No idea," Emily said, sitting down in one of the armchairs scattered along the sides of the room. The woman left, and as the door closed, Emily pulled out her camera. Alone at last.

As she snapped Polaroids of the walls, she grinned. Everything was going her way: She had the pictures, and she had caught Mr. Llewellyn off guard and gotten some important information out of him.

Emily finished the shoot and tucked the camera and the pictures away. She now had three rooms preserved on film, but if she did well (and she intended to do well), they'd be preserved in real life, too.

Her parents had been right: Mr. Llewellyn *was* planning to sell Idlewood to some disrespectful buyer after this last guest-filled weekend, and he was keeping that information to himself for reasons unknown. That was not going to happen. Not if Emily had anything to say about it.

4

THE BEDROOM DOORS were closed when Anna returned to the second-floor hall. Good—the last thing she wanted was another scene. It couldn't be bad to wander the hall, right?

There *had* to be something. No house had a third floor for no good reason. Anna had seen houses that *seemed* like they had another floor, with a series of dummy windows on the roof. But those were different— you could tell there wasn't enough room for another story. With Idlewood, the windows were big. There was another floor, so there had to be a way to access it.

Anna followed the hallway past the themed suites until she reached the sealed doors. Could the entry to the upstairs be past one of them? She pulled on the handle of the first door. Yep. Locked, just like before.

But . . . Anna pulled the key out of her pocket. She found a keyhole but didn't bother trying the key once she saw how small the slot was. The black key was old-fashioned and huge, but this door had a smaller, more modern keyhole.

All of them did. Anna buzzed from door to door, checking each lock. No good. The key didn't have a prayer of fitting in any of them.

Maybe it was a hidden door? Anna smiled. Just like in an ancient tomb! She traced the hall to the bookcase at the end, running her fingers along the pale green wallpaper. All she needed was a crack or raised part, something that signaled a door that had been painted over.

Even though she took her time, stopping at every bump or dent that crossed her fingertips, before long she had circled the whole hall and arrived back in front of the bedrooms. Charlie was sitting on the floor, a notebook on his lap, squinting across the hall.

There it is. He's lost his mind. Anna sat next to him, trying to follow his gaze. The airplane room door? "What are you doing?"

Charlie didn't respond, so Anna asked again and nudged his shoulder. Charlie jumped. His eyes widened when he saw her.

"Sorry," he said. "Deep in thought."

Of course he was. Anna remembered that Charlie had found something strange about the house. "About what?"

Charlie glanced at the door and then at his notebook. Anna could see numbers scribbled on it. Ever the math nerd, her brother. She smirked, and Charlie must have seen it, because he held the notebook against his chest. "Probably nothing," he said.

"You sure?"

"Yep."

"Suit yourself." Anna thought about telling Charlie about her suspicions about the mysterious third floor, but what if she was wrong? Or what if it was totally boring?

Still, Charlie was good at puzzles. Maybe it was time to call that talent into action. She nudged him again. "Hey, want to explore the second floor with me?"

He thought about it, and for a moment Anna thought he might come, but then he shook his head. "Pass. By the way, I forgot to tell you. Mom and Dad say they aren't mad, but they want to talk to you later."

Anna stiffened. No wonder Charlie didn't want to go exploring with her. He probably thought she'd get them both in trouble. Whatever. At least this way, no one could say it was *Charlie's* brains that found the hidden door.

"Okay, then," Anna said. "I'll see you at lunch."

As she stood up, Charlie nodded and laid the notebook flat in his lap again. As she returned to the hallway, Charlie was squinting at the walls.

After tracing the hall another two times, Anna wondered if Charlie was smart not to join this wild-goose chase. Nothing was opening up! Maybe she was wrong about the third floor.

No, no, no! She had seen the windows and the tower, and nothing inside corresponded to them. There *had* to be more to the house, but why was it missing? Had the door been blocked off, walled over?

If so, that was the end of her search. Anna might be willing to cross a rope or pass a DO NOT ENTER sign, but breaking down walls was a little beyond her.

But why wall off a door when there were perfectly good rooms behind it?

Okay, she had to think this through. Walking, tracing the hall for a third time, she barely felt the green wall-paper under her fingers. Instead, she was building a map in her head.

If the rooms went deeper into the house, and the hall bent when the rooms became sealed, then the hall only went part of the way into the house. She tried to remember how big the house was from the outside. Yes. This hall was too short, which meant that if there was a stair or door leading up, it would be—

Right here, she thought, stopping at the bookcase. A thrill tickled her stomach. Of course! If you wanted to hide a door, you put it behind some furniture.

Anna considered the bookcase. It was old and made of dark wood, and it looked heavy. Several books were stacked on the shelves, as well as a plastic succulent that must have been put there when Idlewood started giving tours, but that was it.

Carefully, Anna took the books and set them aside. They were so old, she was afraid that touching them would make the pages crumble. But they stayed intact. She placed them a few feet away from the shelves, patting the cover of the top book (an old copy of *Treasure Island*) to assure herself that they'd be fine there. She also moved the plant, leaving the shelves bare.

Now for the bookcase. Anna almost laughed out loud. It really was like a moment out of a Virginia Maines adventure. When Virginia traveled to France, she found a secret room behind a tapestry in an old castle. It turned out the room was full of old treasures taken during the Crusades. The story had made national news in France. Virginia had been honored by historians in the city. And now, Anna was doing the same thing!

She braced herself along the side of the bookcase and shoved. It didn't budge.

"Huh." Anna stepped back. Odd, that it didn't move at all. As heavy as a bookcase like that would be, it should have at least rocked as she pushed. Anna was only thirteen, but she wasn't weak. She'd just climbed a wall, for crying out loud. But the bookcase didn't move a millimeter.

She moved to the front and grabbed the sides of the bookcase, pulling on them as hard as she could. Nothing moved.

Maybe *this* was what was locked. Anna pulled out the key again and, holding it near her eye, searched the shelves for a keyhole. Maybe it was hidden inside one of the designs carved on the bookcase. That curving line could hide a keyhole . . . no? Maybe it was sneakily placed at the very back, low, almost covered by the shelves. Or not.

After twenty minutes and some frustrated growling, Anna conceded defeat. There was no keyhole anywhere on the bookcase. She moved back to the side and, after counting to three, pushed the bookcase so hard her shoulder popped.

The bookcase didn't even shudder.

Gasping and clutching her aching arm, Anna gingerly picked up the fake plant and books and put them back exactly where she'd found them. After all that work, all that pain, for nothing, she was 100 percent convinced that this bookcase was hiding the entrance to the third floor.

But any secrets hidden up there would have to stay hidden. Because Anna couldn't open the door.

❖ ❖ ❖

A code was like a locked door. As soon as you had the key, it opened easily. Unfortunately for Charlie, he had no idea what the key was.

He had been right: The numbers on the hotel doors were out of order. He'd gone down the hall, up the left side and then down the right, writing each dark, almost-invisible second number into a notebook until he had the following:

3 - 5 - 1 - 18 - 13 - 5 - 15 - 18 - 19 - 1

But what did it mean? At first it seemed like it could be a sequence of odd numbers, but those eighteens threw everything off. Could it be a math equation? A pattern, and the missing numbers were the answer? Or maybe the evens were the clue?

Charlie felt a failure twice over. First, he hadn't managed to drum up the courage to climb that wall when Anna asked him to. Such a coward.

And second, Charlie had blown Anna off when she asked if he wanted to go exploring. That was unlike her—when was the last time she'd asked him to join her adventures? He'd wanted to. But then she smirked, and Charlie remembered: Anna didn't care about codes and numbers. She'd think what he was doing was stupid or boring.

He'd tell her about the code. Just . . . later. Maybe he was completely wrong about this and the numbers really were in a different order a long time ago. If so, he didn't need Anna saying he just needed everything to be a math problem.

The worst thing, Charlie decided, chewing on his pencil, would be if the code was actually straightforward, but you needed to know a key to solve the rest. It could be like the cryptograms in the puzzle books he got for his birthdays. Sometimes, *S* was really the letter *R*, but sometimes it was *A* or *L* or any other letter. If you already knew one, you could figure out the rest. But Charlie didn't have the key.

Or maybe he did. Energized, he tapped his pencil on those number eighteens. Sometimes *S* meant *R*, but in the A1Z26 cipher, where "1" meant "*A*" and "26" meant "*Z*," 18 meant *R*! A commonly used letter in English phrases! And 5 would be *E*, the most common English letter.

Charlie translated the numbers into letters, taking only a moment to make sure that each one was correct before moving on. Now the message read,

CEARMEORSA

Well, that meant nothing. At least, not yet. Charlie was positive he had solved the right code, even though it was gibberish. Look at all those vowels. Look at those *E*s and *A*s and even the *R*s, though they weren't vowels. This didn't look like when he usually failed to correctly solve a code—those were full of strange letters or had no vowels at all (like QXTYDDV), let alone common ones like *E* and *A*, and common consonants like *R*. This looked like a real word. Just not one he'd ever seen before.

Charlie thought and thought until his mom tapped his shoulder and said, "Anna came back a few minutes ago. We're going to lunch."

Charlie welcomed the break. He was sure he'd made the right move in translating the numbers into letters, but that only opened up a new puzzle. Now, he couldn't figure out what the word meant, or if it needed another code to solve.

But he'd solve it. He'd eat a good meal, and he'd go back to the code. The numbers would haunt him until he did.

◆ ◆ ◆

The lunch bell rang, and while Emily took a moment to enjoy the fact that she was *in a place that had an honest-to-goodness lunch bell*, it meant she and her camera had to clear back out of the dining room. She'd gone back in after the elderly couple left so she could get some shots of the furniture, as well as some pictures of the overlook. But when a tour group of elderly women wearing ice-cream-parlor colors and smelling heavily of sunscreen entered the dining room, she had to put her camera away.

The nice-looking woman and her husband, a thin man with a thick beard but a shiny bald head, entered as Emily was leaving and introduced themselves to her as Rosie and Xavier. Rosie gave Emily a wide smile, but Xavier just stared at the girl. A little unnerved, Emily hurried past.

A mustachioed man was coming down the stairs.

"Oh, hello. Enjoying the house?" he asked as Emily passed.

"Yeah," she said. "Sorry. I need to get my parents."

Emily's mom and dad were far back in the upstairs hallway, snapping pictures with the phones they had carefully smuggled inside.

"Hey," Emily said, making them both jump. When they saw it was her, they smiled and put the phones away.

"Be careful," her dad said. "We thought you were Mr. Llewellyn snooping around."

"No, just me," Emily said. "How's the research?"

Her parents glanced at each other and beckoned Emily to follow them into their Rome suite.

"It's promising," her mom said once the door was safely closed. "It's too soon to draft a report to the Virginia Historical Society, but I'm optimistic."

"Me too." Her dad handed Emily his phone, showing her a picture of a big bookcase. "It's a perfect match for the one the Gardners had. This house is untouched, or about as untouched as it can be after so many years."

"If we can document it," her mom said, "we might be able to prove Idlewood should be protected as a historical treasure."

"You'd better work fast," Emily said. "You were right. Mr. Llewellyn is selling the house after this weekend."

Her father looked up from his phone. "How did you find that out?"

"I asked him." Emily smiled.

Her parents did not smile. "What do you mean, you asked him?" her dad asked.

Why weren't they pleased with her? "I didn't ask directly," she said.

"But I'm guessing you got a reaction out of him," her mom said, setting her laptop aside. "Which means he's probably suspicious now."

A twisty, nauseous feeling was growing in Emily's stomach. "Well, maybe, but—"

"Emily, we can't have this! Not again," her mother said. "Losing the house in California was bad enough, but to lose Idlewood, too—"

Emily felt cold prickle over her skin. Northern California. Her parents had been studying the history of an old house, currently a bed-and-breakfast, that some reports said had ties to John Muir. But the house was going to be torn down. The Shaughnessy adults went to visit the house and speak to the owner, but when they did, presenting their case for why the house should be protected and how they thought they could do it, the owner kicked them out. He said he'd rather lose the house than keep pouring money into maintaining the old building and that if he saw them hanging around, he'd call the cops.

Two days later, the house was gone.

And now Idlewood was facing the same problem.

"He's selling the house," Emily said. "Not tearing it down."

"But the company buying it would!" her dad said. "Or they'd strip it and remodel it into some fancy new resort. They won't protect it."

"And now you've made Mr. Llewellyn suspicious of us," her mom added. "What if he finds out what we're trying to do and kicks us out? What hope does Idlewood have then?"

Emily stared past her parents, at the beautiful mural on the wall behind them. It was a bustling Roman marketplace, so detailed Emily could see the dents in a centurion's armor.

So beautiful. And so doomed.

"Okay!" Emily picked up her bag, full of its disguised book and a wad of pictures. "What do you want me to do?"

Her mom sat down on the main room's couch.

"Emmy, we're glad you want to help," she said. "But you're a kid. You should be enjoying the vacation."

"I told you, I want to help," Emily said.

"Like I said, we're grateful. But our timeline just moved up. We only have three days here, and now we can't even count on that. Your father and I need to gather more evidence. We need to show that this house truly hasn't been altered since the days of the Gardners. If we do that, we might be able to convince the Historical Society to step in and protect Idlewood."

"Are you sure it's enough?" Emily asked. She squeezed her bag's strap. "Lots of houses have been kept the same as they were in the past."

Her father shook his head. "Not like this. Most have been remodeled to *look* like they did, not actually stayed the same for so long. Elaine Gardner's order—"

"Yes! Elaine Gardner's order! Why did she make it? Don't you think figuring *that* out is what's going to make this house more than just some old house? Could it because of what Si—"

"Never mind that," her mom said. "We told you, that document doesn't have enough credibility to base our actions on. We have to go on what we can prove." She sighed. "Emily, I understand wanting history to be exciting, but this isn't some silly treasure hunt."

Emily was stung. That wasn't what she was thinking at all!

But her mom was still talking. "It's enough that the house has stayed the same after all these years. It's precious and unique. We'll be able to save it if we can document just how unique it is. We don't need to go looking for a deeper mystery. Sometimes, you do what you can, and that has to be enough."

Her parents were firm. So why bother fighting them? Emily took a deep breath. "Okay. I'm sorry."

Her dad squeezed her shoulder. "We know you're just trying to help. Now let's go to lunch."

Emily wasn't hungry. "You go ahead. I think I'll go downstairs and work on some math homework first."

"Okay, sweetie. After lunch we can . . ." He looked at the itinerary. "Play croquet."

Emily made a face, and he laughed. "Or maybe not. *I* think it could be fun. And it could give us a good look at the outside of the house."

Her mom perked up. "Do you think we could sneak our phones out there?"

As her parents discussed how to best capture Idlewood's facade without anyone seeing, Emily left the room. In the hall, the family with the other kids her age were going down to lunch already. Both the redhead and her brother looked as disgruntled as she felt, although the boy's eyes were far away and he bumped into the stair's bannister.

Emily rolled her eyes and followed them downstairs. *They don't get it*, she thought. Sure, Idlewood was old and special, but not many people thought that mattered anymore. There were lots of old houses. But people liked mysteries. There was a history here, surrounding why Mrs. Gardner had ordered the house to remain as it was. Maybe her parents could save Idlewood by showing how alike it was to the original. *Maybe.* But if not, Emily would be ready with her own pictures, with evidence pointing to a reason why Mrs. Gardner wanted the house kept pristine. The papers hidden in Emily's book would guide her. It didn't matter that Mr. Llewellyn was suspicious; a kid could move around without people paying too much attention. Or, well, maybe not, she thought, remembering the redhead's "arrest" that morning.

But still, Emily wasn't stupid, and she wasn't useless. She'd show her parents that she was right and that this house's fate hinged on learning why Mrs. Gardner had made her order. While her parents were out playing croquet, Emily would find the evidence she was looking for.

Emily sat in the entry hall, "math" book on her lap, and waited for the other family to go inside the dining room, followed by her parents, before she took a few pictures of the walls and furniture. She opened her book on a whim, to the pages that showed the entry hall back when Idlewood belonged to the Gardner family.

The house really had stayed the same. Looking at the black-and-white pictures in the book and then at the room around her, Emily could see no difference besides the color.

No, wait. There was one difference. Emily glanced down at a picture of the carved door with its dragon statues. *Statues*, plural, one on each side. But now, one of the big, heavy statues was on the *other* side of the room.

Emily frowned. Was this a clue to the past? Making sure no one was watching, she snapped pictures of both statues to study later. Mrs. Gardner had wanted the house to stay the same, in every way. If Emily and her parents were ever going to understand Mrs. Gardner's reasons for that demand, then these details mattered. The statue had probably been moved when Mr. Llewellyn corrected the original builders' "errors."

Emily rose from the chair, leaving her book tented over her camera, and approached the carved door. It would be locked, of course. But Emily didn't care about going inside. Instead, she knelt by the bare spot on the other side.

Just as she thought: The ground was etched with notches where this bronze Chinese dragon statue had once been. Well, if she was going to save Idlewood, then she should start by honoring the memory of the people who built it, and she could do *that* by moving a statue back to where it was supposed to be.

Emily looked around. The room was empty. It was just her, the statues, and her task.

It wasn't easy. The big, heavy statue made a scratching sound as Emily pulled it, so she had to waddle it over to prevent damaging the floor. It also caught on every rug, so Emily had to stop, pull the rug back, shove the statue past, and then replace the rug. Once she got it across the room, she had to turn it around and maneuver it into the notches on the ground.

"Come on, you," she grunted, giving it one last push.

The statue jolted a few inches, landing in the notches with a satisfying click that seemed to resonate deep in the stone and echo through the foundation of the house.

"Good." Emily sat beside the statue and wiped the sweat from her forehead. Moving a statue wouldn't change the world, but it was a start. She looked at the two dragons, right next to each other. Was it important that they stay together?

She'd come back and figure it out later. Now, lunch. She'd worked up an appetite moving the statue, and the smell of roasted ham floated out of the dining room, making Emily's stomach growl. So she took a few more pictures (with the statue in the right place now) and ran her camera and book back to her room before joining her parents for an authentic 1920s lunch.

◆ ◆ ◆

Anna hadn't really cared for lunch. It was ham sandwiches and some salad loaded with cottage cheese. She would have preferred spaghetti, but her parents liked the old-fashioned food from an old-fashioned time, and that made them happy, which meant they gave her a quick "don't do it again" lecture about going through other people's rooms before turning back to their meals.

Charlie wasn't much fun, either. Anna had to shake him out of his thoughts to get him talking, but before long, he was lost in his own world again. Not even mentioning the library was enough to keep him in the present.

The only other thing to do was listen to the other

guests introduce themselves to one another. The couple Anna had spotted outside (the ones with the little bundle), their sport sunglasses pushed up on their foreheads, were talking to the Matching T-Shirts family, and two single guests, Pins-All-Over-Suitcase Man and the Book Lady, had chosen seats next to each other and were having a fevered conversation in low voices. The woman had one of her books on her lap. This one was titled *DNA Coding for Fun and Profit.*

The slew of old women in pastel shorts and blouses were buzzing in and out of the room so often that Anna couldn't count them. What room could fit all of them (and the thick fog of coconut scent they carried with them)?

Anna's parents were busy talking to the couple from the airplane room.

"This is a nice house," Mr. Mustache was telling them. "But I think the weather is too wet here."

"Not good for the respiratory system," his wife, Quilted Bag, said, waving a hand at her throat. "That time we visited Key Largo was much more invigorating. Still, the trees are lovely."

"Why come, then?" Anna's father asked.

Mr. Mustache settled back in his chair. "Contest winners," he said, patting his wife's arm. "We enter so many contests for vacations. That's how we went to Key Largo. And when I looked up the history of Idlewood, I wanted to come see it for myself."

"It's also nice to get away," Quilted Bag said. "I work at a publishing house. It can get intense."

"Winners, huh?" Anna's mom smiled. "Well, as a matter of fact, so are we."

Great. This again.

No one seemed to want to talk to Anna herself, not even Mr. Mustache's wife, who smiled from across the table and offered Anna a butterscotch candy from her colorful bag as her husband and Anna's mom spoke. So Anna finished lunch and then ran outside, sticking the candy in her pocket. Garrett the Gateman was out there, setting up wickets for croquet. Anna's parents were planning on playing croquet after lunch, but Anna's own plans included vanishing until the game was over.

Garrett waved at her and called out, "How's your first day here? Having lots of fun?" But she just waved and ran past.

Anna explored the grounds, finding an evergreen maze behind the house, but as she wandered to the maze, she realized she kept raising her eyes to that elusive third floor.

No. There had to be a way to get there. An explorer didn't give up just because something was hard. Virginia Maines wouldn't have found that French treasure room if she wasn't persistent. Anna must have missed something.

Annoyed, she turned away from the maze and hurried back into the house. The dark-haired snob's parents were examining a vase and leaped away, looking startled, as Anna marched by. Why were all the adults so jumpy around her?

Anna marched to the big bookcase on the second

floor. Without removing the books this time, she wrapped her fingers around one side of the shelves, like she was about to pull on a door. With a grunt, she pulled.

And with a click and a squeak, the bookcase swung open on a hinge. Anna almost fell over. It worked! She thought she'd pulled like that before, but apparently she hadn't.

She pushed the door open. A staircase, lined with a rug that must have once been beautiful but was now gray with dust, stretched up to the third floor.

The air seemed heavy, muffling the sounds of people going back to their rooms after lunch or heading out to claim their balls and mallets. This was what it felt like to see something no one had seen in a long time. This was what it felt like to be a real explorer.

Anna closed the door behind her and climbed the dusty stairs.

5

CHARLIE HAD a very strange afternoon, but that was his own fault. After lunch with his parents and a distracted and annoyed Anna (his parents had given her a short lecture about going where she wasn't allowed), his parents tried to convince him to play croquet.

"It will be fun," his mother said. "Anna's probably already out there."

Charlie sincerely doubted it. Hitting a ball around the lawn with a mallet didn't seem wild enough for Anna. He guessed she was probably long gone into the woods, and they wouldn't see her until dinner.

"I think I'll sit this one out," he said. "Maybe I'll find that library Anna told me about."

"You sure?" his dad said, and, when Charlie nodded, simply added, "We'll do something together as a family tomorrow, then. Maybe a hike."

They left, and Charlie took his notebook and did just as he'd said: He found the library.

The room, though big, felt cramped with all the closely packed shelves of books. Yellowed light shone through old glass, illuminating specks of dust floating in the air, and in the center of the room stood a dark wood podium with a huge, open book on it. Ignoring the book (for now), Charlie sat in a brocaded armchair and took a deep breath, inhaling the woody smell of the library. Later, he'd browse a little. But for now, he had to get back to solving the code.

CEARMEORSA

Plenty of vowels, common letters. Could they just be in the wrong order? It was worth looking into. Charlie wrote down every possible anagram he could think of using the letters from the code.

Some were really out there (*race me soar*), but some seemed to make a little more sense. *Area comers?* That could make sense, since the house had been a hotel. But if that was the answer, what could it possibly mean?

Charlie looked at the other answers. *Cease armor? Camera rose? Cameo rears?* Wasn't there a kind of old-fashioned jewelry called a cameo? In this old-fashioned house, maybe he could find one. Same with armor. There was a sword hanging over his bed. Maybe another room had the suit of armor it belonged to.

But where? Charlie packed up his notebook, with his top anagrams circled. It looked like he'd have to go on a hunt. But for what? He'd just have to hope he'd know whatever it was when he saw it. Still, he'd find nothing if he didn't go out and look.

When he left the library, he looked at the other doors along the hall, so much like the ones upstairs with their misplaced numbers. What if the next clue was in someone else's suite? Somewhere off-limits?

Anna wouldn't hesitate. She'd stomp right over to the room with the clue and go inside by any means necessary. She'd get in trouble, but she'd get it done.

Charlie swallowed hard and marched upstairs. He stopped at the first door on the right. Raising a hand, he prepared to knock on the door but then stepped back and scurried down the stairs. This wasn't running away, he told himself. The clues could just as easily be downstairs in the public rooms.

He searched the dining room, the parlor, and the library—no suits of armor or cameo jewelry, though there was a woman with thick, curly gray hair running her hands over the furniture in the parlor. Odd—and even odder when she knelt down and looked under a sofa. Was she part of the big group of women staying here this weekend? He didn't notice a sunscreen smell.

The indoor greenhouse, while really cool, had nothing, either. He got chased out of the kitchen when he went looking for "cream arose," which he interpreted to mean "whipped cream." It seemed the cook didn't agree.

Charlie sat in the entry hall, fiddling with his glasses and wondering if it was time to ask the other guests for a tour of their rooms. But the idea made his skin crawl. What if he asked and one of the guests didn't want him seeing the room, or kept some doors locked? It would be the last try; if one of the guests wouldn't let him in, and the next clue was inside, that was the end of it. Charlie couldn't sneak in if he got turned down—even imagining it made him want to turn himself in to Mr. Llewellyn. The puzzle would remain unsolved forever, and Charlie would never find out why it had existed in the first place. Who put a code on hotel doors?

No. He *had* to find out. Charlie searched the entry hall. Maybe something in here would be the clue he was looking for.

His eyes landed on the carved door between the two dragon statues. (Hadn't one of the statues been across the room before?) The door was carved with all kinds of flowers, like lilies, poppies, and roses. Some of the anagrams he'd figured out had included the word *rose*. A cream rose. Camera rose.

Without taking his eyes off the door, Charlie got up and walked to it. Right in the center of the door was a carved bouquet that included several roses.

He ran his fingers over them. The wood felt cool and very smooth. Worn down from lots of people touching it? Pressing it? Charlie pushed down on one rose. Nothing moved. So he pushed on another one, with the same result.

Wait. "*Camera* rose." Maybe the roses weren't switches. Maybe they were convenient places to hide little cameras.

Charlie leaned into the carved tangle of petals, searching for a glint of a glass lens in the warm brown wood. Why would someone put a camera in the roses?

"Ahem."

Charlie spun around to see the man with the beard and bald head from down the hall. He was the husband of the lady with the graying hair. What was his name? The lady was Rosie; they'd all introduced themselves at lunch, though Charlie didn't remember most of the names.

"What are you doing?" the thin man asked.

"Looking for hidden cameras," Charlie said, then mentally scolded himself. Why did he say that? Now the man would laugh or have more questions than Charlie could answer.

The bald man didn't laugh. He leaned closer. "Did you find one?"

Charlie stepped back to allow the man to look. "No."

"Then why do you think there is one?"

Good question. "I don't know." Charlie wasn't ready to give up the code. But the man was acting odd, and Charlie pulled at the loose thread. "Why do *you* think there's one?"

The man stepped back and laughed. "Got me there. It's an old house. Makes sense that Mr. Llewellyn would have ways to watch over his property. I'm Xavier, by the way."

"Charlie. Isn't there croquet right now?"

"Not really my style." Xavier looked around. "I'd

better find my wife. The Appalachian Trail bends close to the house, and we thought we'd take a hike instead of the scheduled activity. Though if you ask me, I would prefer to stay inside and read a book." The bald man gave Charlie a quick smile and left.

Charlie looked at the carved door one more time and abandoned it quickly. The code didn't say *camera rose*. The house was renovated into a hotel in the 1930s, and Charlie didn't think they had cameras small enough to hide in a wooden rose back then. And that was when the code would have been set in the numbered doors.

Huh. Two dragon statues. The other had been across the room. How had it moved?

That was a puzzle for another day. For now, Charlie turned his attention to the code. There had to be a clear way to read it. No one set a code that *nobody* was supposed to be able to solve. Maybe he should follow Xavier's example and read a book, just to clear his head.

Wait. A book. When Charlie had written down the numbers, he'd written them by following the hallway all the way around, starting down the left side and coming back up the right, ending in the same place. But what if he had them in the wrong order? What if he was supposed to read them like the pages of a book: left, right, left, right, following how the doors' new numbers counted up?

Charlie went back upstairs to the doors. Starting on the left and going back and forth down the hall, he wrote down the numbers again.

3-1-5-19-1-18-18-15-13-5

Here goes nothing. Charlie translated the numbers into letters, fingers shaking with excitement.

CAESARROME

Success!

"Caesar Rome. Caesar Rome!" he said out loud, waving the notebook. Then he stopped, suddenly aware that he was in a public area.

Finally, the message made sense. But what did it *mean*?

Maybe he should go back to the library. There might be a book about Julius Caesar there. But so far the code had always been simpler than he'd expected. He'd caused himself more trouble than needed by overthinking the problem. So maybe he'd already been given the key to understanding the code. Maybe the placement of the code was part of the code. The numbers were on the suite doors, so perhaps the doors themselves were the key. Or the suites were.

Charlie looked around at the closed doors on either side of the hallway. The Hendersons were staying in the China suite, and from Anna's explorations earlier, he knew the other suites were themed. What were the rest, and was one of them Rome?

Yes. One had to be Rome. Charlie didn't know which suite it was, but a few knocks and polite inquiries would get him there.

He'd solved the code. Now it was time to go to Rome.

It took Charlie a few doors to find it. He'd knocked on one, interrupting a couple who were . . . very much into each other in a Pacific Islands room, but they were friendly enough to let him look around. Another knock led to a lady with lots of dark hair and a book in her hand (*A Brief History of Tomatoes*), who insisted he come back later with his parents to see her room—the Amazon suite—as she was about to take a nap. Which was odd, because he swore he could hear someone else's voice from in there.

When he did find the right suite, the person who opened the door was the girl who had bothered Anna earlier. "What do you want?" she asked.

Charlie glanced around her and saw the marble statues and painted walls. Yep. Rome. He turned his attention back to the girl.

She was about his age and wore her hair in her face. Her voice was quiet, and she seemed shy. At least, all the markers were there: the posture, the voice, the hair. But something was wrong with that image. The girl's voice, though quiet, was steely, and Charlie had seen her showing off earlier.

This was an act. But why?

Like the dragon statues, it was another puzzle to save for later. "I'd like to see your suite," he said. "If it's all right."

The girl eyed him. "Why?"

He shrugged. "The suites are themed. I want to see them all. I won't be a problem, I swear."

"You're the kid they say won a place here. Math contest?"

Charlie blushed. Maybe he should have paid more attention to what his parents had been saying during lunch. "Yeah. It's embarrassing, I know."

"Why?"

He looked at her.

She shrugged. "I mean, why be embarrassed? If you like something so much, why not own it?"

"You sound like you know from experience."

"Maybe a little. I'm a bit of a geek myself."

Charlie smiled, and the girl grinned back. This was promising. "So, can I look around?"

The girl's smile dropped. She glanced back into the suite, then at Charlie. "Um, well, my parents just left to go play croquet. And . . . I'm supposed to meet them."

"Oh." Charlie's heart sank. "I can come back later, I guess. Maybe I'll come with you to play croquet. My parents are down there, too."

"No, no! It's fine," she said. "It's fine. What's your name?"

"Charlie."

"I'm Emily. So, Charlie, um, you can come in. I can trust you, right?"

Charlie nodded, making his glasses slip down his nose. He pushed them up. "I'll be in and out."

"Okay. I guess it's okay. Just . . . hold on a moment."

Charlie waited as the girl, Emily, closed the door. He could hear her bustling around inside the room. "Okay," she said, opening the door again. A huge bag hung from her shoulder, and a brown-paper-covered math book poked out of it. "There," she said. "I'm on my way. Just . . . be careful, okay? And close the door when you leave." Her eyes were wide.

Again, Charlie felt the tug of something that didn't make sense, and again he filed it away for later. You couldn't get distracted by one puzzle while in the middle of another one. It would divide brain energy.

So he nodded, smiled, and watched as Emily left. Bringing a math book on vacation? Maybe he'd found a kindred spirit in her.

Then he turned to face the suite. Time to work.

The entry room of the Rome suite was exquisite. The furniture was in purple and gold, and there were white pillars at each corner. The rest of the furniture was sparse, allowing people to see the beautiful Roman cityscape painted on the walls.

The code had said *Caesar Rome*. He was in Rome, so it made sense that the emperor would be here, too. Charlie searched the entry room, and then every other room, for pictures or statues of Julius Caesar. Not one. He even went into the master bedroom (feeling very awkward, as this was parental space) and found nothing besides a couple of suitcases (which he didn't touch) and some history books (stacked under the bed) about the 1920s and the explorer Virginia Maines.

Interesting. That was Anna's favorite explorer.

But no Caesar. No busts, statues, or anything. He'd

even checked the baseboards and the people in the Roman cityscape painting, searching for anyone who looked like the pictures he'd seen of Julius Caesar. He'd turned up nothing, which was weird. Who thought of Rome and *didn't* also think of Caesar?

Charlie wandered the suite, his footsteps echoing in the emptiness. Who knew how long that emptiness would last? Emily and her family could come back any minute now. They couldn't find him here! He said he'd be in and out. Staying so long, poking around, looked suspicious. What would he say?

What would Anna do? Mouth off, probably. But she wouldn't be afraid. So *he* shouldn't be afraid.

Easier said than done. Maybe it would help if he focused on the search, one last time.

With a huff, Charlie fell into the purple couch in the entry room. His eyes roamed the painted walls. One of the faces there could be Caesar; it wasn't like he had the man's face memorized.

Or maybe he was stuck on the wrong idea. Charlie took off his glasses, letting the world turn into a blur. Clear the slate. Start again.

He put the glasses back on and stared at the painting. Time passed. He needed to find his clue. If Emily's family came back, he might be able to leave without getting into trouble, but he wouldn't get another chance to come in.

It really was a beautiful, intricate painting. Not something you'd expect as a mural in a hotel suite. There were people on the streets of Rome, with a blue sky and light brown buildings. The faces of the people had been painted clearly, and everything, down to the last pin on a person's robes and individual blades of grass, had been carefully stroked in.

Charlie sat up. So clear, so intricate, you could probably read the signs if there were any.

And there were! Leaping up from the couch, Charlie ran to the painting. Near the door was the beginning of the road that passed through Rome, and beside it was a stone sign. The sign's words, carved in simple cuts, were not in English or Latin. They were a jumble of letters:

TCOY DQO SDNO

Another code! Charlie jotted the letters down in his notebook. He stood up and stepped back, taking in the whole painting.

It was like putting on his glasses. There, painted in tiny strokes on the hem of a man's toga, was TQOD-SUQO. And a guard near a graffitied wall was gesturing at ESIDKG with a key.

The key. Caesar Rome. There was no Caesar here (which was a clue in itself), but there *was* a kind of code called a Caesar cipher. It used a shifted alphabet, sometimes moving the letters up or back. Shifting the alphabet "four ahead," for example, would make A=E, B=F, and so on until Z=D. But a "keyed Caesar" was a specific variation that used a code word to "unlock" the cipher. For example, if Charlie used his own name as the key, all the letters of his name would go first, and the shifted alphabet would look like:

CHARLIEBDFGJKMNOPQSTUVWXYZ

So, C=A, H=B, and so on. If a letter in the code word repeated, you just skipped it. For example, if he used his full name, "Charlie Henderson," the alphabet would be:

CHARLIENDSOBFGJKMPQTUVWXYZ

You'd remove all the repeated letters from "Charlie Henderson" until his last name was just "NDSO." After all, you could only have twenty-six letters in an English alphabet, or it wouldn't work.

The guard there, with his painted key, seemed to prove that this was a keyed cipher, not just a shifted alphabet.

It made sense. Charlie looked back at the mural's other phrases. The sign had a tiny key painted on its side, and the man's toga had another key hanging from it.

A new challenge. So what was the key that would turn the jumble of letters in the mural into a readable message?

Charlie searched the painting for any other words, in English, hoping they might give him the code word. No use. He was going to have to use trial and error to guess what it might be.

But he would. As Charlie left the Roman room, carefully closing the door behind him, his determination grew. He'd already managed to solve so much of the code. Nothing was going to stop him from figuring out the rest!

6

THE DUSTY STAIRS to the third floor were silent as Anna ascended, the bookcase door closed behind her. The layers of dust cushioned her steps, making her feel like a ghost floating along.

At the top of the stairs was a long hallway. It was dark and smelled musty, and Anna had to cover her nose and mouth to keep from coughing and sneezing. She didn't know how thin the walls (or ceiling) were, and she didn't want to get caught. Again.

The carpet stretched down the hall. Mouse droppings littered the ground, and cobwebs bridged the walls to the ceiling overhead. No one had been here, not for years and years.

The silent air felt heavy with the weight of what this third floor had been a long time ago but wasn't anymore. Who had lived here? Why had it been blocked off but not walled off for good?

Anna tiptoed down the hall and stopped at the first room. She laid her hand on its dusty door handle, soft and slick beneath her fingers. If she had a floor of a building that was off-limits, she'd seal all the doors so no one could get in. But what if . . .

She turned the handle. The door opened, creaking as she pushed it. Inside was a bedroom with a huge brass bed frame pressed against the wall. The metal had corroded, turning green, and the mattress was gone. There was also a dresser, which, when Anna checked it, was totally empty.

She went to the window. Pale light shone through the dingy glass, and down below the other guests were playing croquet. Her own parents were down there, playing as a team. Her mom hit the ball into the pond. Charlie was nowhere to be seen. Anna stepped away from the window and went to the closet.

It was empty except for a dress, which had been left hanging on a hook inside the door. Once it had been pale blue, with a deep neckline (wasn't the past supposed to be all proper, Anna wondered?) and a skirt that looked like it would be fun to twirl in. But now the blue was barely visible beneath the dust, and in places the color had bleached and faded to a gross yellow. There were holes where moths had nibbled the fabric. She touched the dress, the cloth silky under her fingers.

"Who did you belong to?" Anna breathed, and then coughed on the dust swirling around her, loosened from the dress by her touch. Mr. Llewellyn had given the family a history of Idlewood, but Anna hadn't had a chance to read it before the upstairs mystery took all her attention.

She rubbed the cloth gently between her hands. It must have been an expensive dress. For a moment, Anna considered taking it with her, as proof that she'd found this place. But that would be wrong. The dress wasn't hers. It belonged here, on this dusty secret floor. And Anna was no thief.

Anna closed the closet and left the room. She closed the door behind her and made her way to the next room. Each room was like the last: old, dusty, and empty. Here and there, she found remnants of the family that used to live in the house. A few hairpins. A man's shoe. Out in the hall, on a chair, was a stack of books. Anna picked up the top one. Its cover had been torn off, but it still looked familiar. She set it back down and kept exploring.

At the end of the hall, Anna turned left and discovered another long hall. This one had no doors on either side, but there was one down at the end. Anna's heart sped up as she ran to the door.

But when she pulled on the handle, it didn't move. Another locked door.

Anna took out the tarnished key she'd found and set it to the lock. It didn't go in at all, so that was another dead end. Literally.

She sighed and looked around. The door to the third floor had been hidden, so maybe there was more than met the eye here, too. Anna took a step back and examined the door.

The door itself looked like all the others in the house, except for the carved one downstairs: big, wooden, flat. But while the other doors were set in painted plaster walls, this one was set in gray stones, like the outside of the house.

Hmm. That did make sense. If Anna's mental map was correct, this hallway connected to the house's tower. Maybe the tower had been separate once, and the hallway was added later to connect the rest of the house to it through this door.

But if it was the same stone as the outside, maybe it was just as easy to climb. Ideas sparking, Anna set her hand on the stone. The dust coated her hands, like a gymnast's chalk. Yes! They were just as rough as the stones she'd climbed earlier that morning. But was there a ledge, like outside?

Anna looked up and choked on dust. Her coughing and spluttering turned to laughter, echoing in the empty hall. "Oh my gosh," she said. "What kind of house is this?"

A hole had been cut into the ceiling, just above the handholds Anna had found. A hole meant to accommodate a climber.

Anna had a sudden vision of a rich lady in diamonds and that blue dress from the closet clambering up through the hole and snorted.

Okay, so maybe not her. The husband, then? Who needed this kind of entrance to the tower when there was a perfectly good door?

Only one way to find out. Anna couldn't have ignored this mystery even if her parents, Charlie, and Mr. Llewellyn had begged her to. She rubbed her hands on her dusty clothes (there was no way to avoid it—it stuck to everything) and began the climb.

It wasn't any harder than the climbing stones outside. Anna lifted herself into a small room, cut off from the rest of the house, with unpainted walls. There was a small door in front of her. Very small.

"Alice in Wonderland," she whispered, kneeling in front of it. The knob turned with a squeak, and soon Anna was crawling through the little door into the most marvelous room she'd ever seen.

It was the inside of the tower. A spiral staircase wound around the stone outside, leading from the ground floor where Anna stood to several platforms above. Ropes hung from the platforms to the ground, or stretched to the walls. Like the other rooms, this tower room was covered with dust. But unlike the others, this room wasn't emptied of its belongings. Items littered the ground: books, a few plates and cups, and stacks of loose papers.

Anna stepped tentatively inside. The stone walls were plastered with maps and charts. The paper had yellowed with time, but the images were unmistakable: India, China, Africa. A map of the Pacific Ocean hung over an old, dusty sofa.

Anna raised a hand to touch the Pacific Ocean map but stopped. She didn't want to destroy anything. Still, who had lived here? This room seemed different from the other rooms on the third floor. Those had belonged to a proper, wealthy lady and her gentleman husband. This tower was messy, lived in. Forgotten.

Maybe this was an office of some kind. Anna had no idea what kind of man Mr. Gardner was—maybe he was a sea captain or traveler in his own right. But it wasn't like any office she'd ever seen.

Anna climbed the creaky stairs to the platforms above. On the first one, she found a locked chest. On the next, a wardrobe. When she looked inside, she found both women's dresses and men's jackets and pants made of heavy material.

Maybe both Gardners used the tower? If so, they were much more interesting people than Anna had expected.

And those ropes . . . some stretched taut like tight-ropes, between the platforms and the walls, and others held wooden slats, like seats on swings. What were they for?

Anna climbed all the way to the top and found a place that looked like it could be Rapunzel's tower room. The small, topmost platform held a little bed and a desk that overlooked one window. This bed was made with a red comforter—or at least, it would have been red once. Sunlight had bleached much of the cloth, leaving only a few dark patches on the side of the bed away from the window. There, even under the dust frosting the bed, the vibrant color shone through.

"Who used you?" she asked.

The third floor had felt heavy with memories, but here, the atmosphere felt more alive to Anna. There, the rooms had been packed up and moved away, with small remnants left behind. Tombs. But this room was full and busy, like the owner had just gone down to dinner and would be back. Eventually.

She pulled out the dusty chair and sat at the desk. Out the window, she could see the tops of the trees around Idlewood blowing in the wind. They looked like a stormy green sea, making a wooden roof of a nearby building look like a raft. Interesting. Anna had thought there weren't any other buildings in the area. Maybe it was a work shed, for Garrett the Gateman.

Back to the desk. A desk could hold all kinds of mysteries. Anna had once searched her father's desk and found all of her and Charlie's baby teeth. She wondered why he'd kept them. It wasn't like he could *do* anything with them.

What secrets did this desk hold? Hopping out of the chair, Anna rattled the handles on the desk's drawers, dislodging dust and causing another coughing fit. Eyes streaming, she grabbed an old piece of cloth off the ground and dusted the desk as well as she could. The sun-bleached wood was marred with scratches and even a few small burns.

Whoever owned this used it hard, she thought. She pulled on one of the drawers, and it opened.

Inside were an envelope, a compass, and a gold picture frame. Anna took out the compass first. It was old and heavy, cased in tarnished brass. She spun it in her hands and noted with satisfaction that even after all these years, it still pointed north.

Then she pulled out the envelope. Letters were just what she needed: names, reasons for this house and its secret third floor—and who had lived here in this tower.

Carefully, treating the old paper like it could dissolve in her hands at any moment, Anna unfolded the letter and laid it on the cleaned desk.

The letter was dated March 14, 1921.

My dear Ginny,
I know this letter may find you rather late, but I couldn't wait until you were back to tell you the good news. Everett has proposed, and I have accepted. I will now be the new Mrs. Gardner of Idlewood.

So this was written by Mrs. Gardner, Anna realized. She wouldn't have kept her own letters, so the room must have belonged to "Ginny." Anna kept reading.

I'm pleased to be getting married, as I'm sure you know, not only because Everett is a wonderful, handsome man but because I can finally shed my ridiculous rhyming name. See? Now you're laughing! It never seemed fair that you should get the only elegant name in the family, especially since you have no use for anything elegant in your life. As for Idlewood, it's a lovely house, and I think you will like it as much as I do. Yes, it is elegant. But it is also spacious and rather remote, deep in the forests in the mountains here, and although it's not the kind of adventure I'm sure you're used to, it is plenty for me.

Speaking of adventures, I have recently finished reading a lovely book by an English lady named Agatha Christie. I have high hopes for her, and for her Monsieur Poirot. When you come home for the wedding (which you will have to!), we shall have a discussion about it. With its clues and mystery, I think you will enjoy it.

The wedding will be in July. You must be there. I cannot get married without my sister beside me! I expect your reply or your presence soon.

With love,

Elaine Maines (Soon to be Gardner!)

Anna's heart stopped. As she'd read, she had pieced together an image of Mrs. Gardner curled up in Idlewood's library, writing this letter, although at that point, she probably hadn't lived here yet, and of Ginny, the sister. An adventurer. A traveler. But then came the last name. Maines. Elaine Maines. Ginny Maines.

Virginia Maines.

Fingers trembling, Anna scrambled for the picture frame in the drawer. No. It couldn't be. There was no way that Anna could be this lucky, that she could be in the same place where the one and only, the mysterious and vanished, explorer of all explorers—

There was the picture. And there she was, dark hair as curly as Anna's own, wearing a sturdy-looking dress and a smirk, eyes twinkling even in the old picture.

Her arm was thrown around another young woman. Elaine.

It was her. Anna's breathing quickened, and her hands tightened on the frame. Virginia Maines had been here. Had lived here, in this tower! No wonder it was so hard to get to—the woman lived for adventure. Those ropes and swings must have been for practice, or just letting off steam. Anna would have designed her own tower the exact same way.

She turned back to the letter and read it again with her new perspective. How had Virginia come to have this tower room? What happened? And had this been the place where she had vanished, leaving behind all her things like treasures in a pharaoh's tomb?

The letter was dated in 1921. Virginia had disappeared without a trace in 1925. Four years later.

Anna sat back and looked out the window. Virginia Maines. Oh, man. The things these walls had seen. If they could talk—

What if they could? There were so many things spread around—what if Virginia had left a clue behind about what happened to her? The room was filthy; the Gardners had locked it up. Somewhere in all this mess could lie a treasure.

Where to start? Letters. There had to be more letters!

Anna rifled through the desk drawer but found nothing else. She looked around. The tower was a mess of papers. If Virginia had kept one letter, chances were good she had kept more. Maybe they were scattered in the stacks.

No time to lose—she had to find out more! But as she stood to begin her search, she heard the distant sound of the dinner bell. Darn it! Her parents were going to wonder where she'd been. Anna raced down the stairs and out of the tower, trailing clouds of dust all the way.

As she hurried down the third-floor hall, back to the stairs and the bookcase door, she realized she was going to have to shower or everyone was going to know she'd been poking around where she wasn't allowed. She sighed.

Looked like she'd be late for dinner.

7

DINNER WAS chicken and potatoes, served with all the guests sitting around the dining room. The tables were large enough to accommodate everyone, but the adults had started to mingle, leaving Emily to sit with the other kids her age.

Mr. Llewellyn was chatting with the women's tour group. He leaned back slightly, probably due to the thick cloud of coconut sunblock around them. Emily's parents sat nearby, looking preoccupied but listening in. Another couple with sport sunglasses perched on their heads had been chatting pleasantly to a lady with dark hair tied back in a braid.

Another family had five kids, all under the age of six, so their mom sat with them at one table in the nice, blue dining room, keeping the youngest's hands off the white linen tablecloths. They were all wearing the same T-shirts with a cutesy Idlewood slogan on them. One of the kids wandered over to the Sunglasses Woman and opened her purse, pulling out a dark tan cookie and raising it to her mouth. The woman snatched it out of the child's hand, shoved it back in the purse, and scolded the child, making her cry.

As for the kids Emily's age, the redhead and the boy with glasses, they had also opted to sit apart from their parents. Though, neither of them seemed like they were in any mood to talk.

The boy, Charlie, kept mumbling to himself, jotting things down in a notebook, then frowning and staring ahead like he could see into another dimension. And the girl fidgeted with her fork, her food, her hair (wet, Emily noticed—she must have gone into the pond) and kept glancing back at the door to the entry hall.

No matter, Emily thought. She wasn't here to play anyway. She had work to do and was almost done. Backing out of croquet with her parents had been smart. While they'd snuck photos of the facade, she had managed to photograph the entrance hall. Leaving Charlie to explore her family's suite had been a gamble, but she'd taken the real evidence with her (the book, photos, and some of her parents' notes were still in her bag) and pushed the somewhat less suspicious books under a bed. He wouldn't have noticed anything.

Besides, she couldn't have let him follow her, not when she wasn't actually going outside. It was much safer to leave him there while she did her work.

Two more days. Emily looked at her half-eaten food.

She'd gotten all the pictures, but what could she do with two more days?

Find absolute proof that Idlewood should not be torn down. Her parents had come to prove that Idlewood was perfectly preserved enough to be protected. But Emily would prove why it had been preserved. She had her theories based on unsubstantiated notes from her parents, but if she could find proof, everything would be fixed. It would be a historic site, and the Shaughnessys would have grounds to have it protected. But they only had the rest of the weekend to find that proof before Mr. Llewellyn's sale of the house went into effect and new owners demolished the house or ruined it some other way. They might not care about history. But Emily did.

And just imagine! If she were the one to unlock it all, her parents would finally know she had what it took to be a historian like them.

Sitting silent among so many people was getting a little old. Emily turned to the boy sitting next to her. "Hey, Charlie."

He jumped like she'd poked him with her fork. "What?"

She smiled at him. "How did you like the Rome suite?"

"Um, I really liked it. The paintings on the walls were really neat."

"I think so, too. What did you like about them?"

Charlie reddened. "I don't know. There was . . . just a lot to look at, you know?"

He peered at her through his glasses, which made her

feel a little like a specimen under dual magnifying lenses. "I guess. I've been pretty busy."

"Busy doing what? You can't play croquet all day."

Emily scowled. "None of your business."

"Fine." He shrugged. "I thought if we were interested in something, we were supposed to own it, right?"

"Yeah, but . . . that's different."

They sat in a silence broken only by the ambient chatter of dinner. Then Charlie said, "By any chance, have you seen anything like a key in your rooms?"

"A key?" Emily asked at the same time as the red-head. "What kind of key?" the other girl continued.

Charlie shook his head. "I don't know, Anna. Probably not a real one. A picture. I . . . I heard about old-fashioned Roman keys beings really cool, and I thought the Roman room might have something like that."

"Oh," Anna said, shifting in her seat. Her eyes flicked up at the ceiling, back at the door, and then down to her plate.

"I'll keep an eye out," Emily said. "But I haven't seen one yet. Old keys are pretty cool, though," she added. "The Romans used to wear them on their fingers because they didn't have pockets."

Charlie's eyes lit up. "That *is* pretty cool. I wonder if they ever put them on the wrong finger and got them stuck there."

Emily laughed. "Maybe."

"Um, Emily, right?" This was the redhead, Anna. "You know a lot about history?"

"A bit," Emily said, though she allowed the truth of *yes, I know a heck of a lot* to slide into her voice.

Charlie heard it. "Is history your thing, then?"

Emily gave a modest shrug. "It interests me. So I pick up some interesting facts."

"Not math, then," Charlie said, looking back at his dinner.

But Anna's eyes gleamed. "What do you know about Idlewood?" she asked. "Before dinner, I read the little history they gave us, but it wasn't a lot."

Emily snorted. "No, it isn't."

"So you know more, then? What happened here? When, and why?"

Oh, those were some interesting questions. Emily could tell a lot. She could talk about Mr. and Mrs. Gardner and how they met and how the sister of a famous lady explorer had come to be a rich man's wife, and maybe she could even regale them with what she thought of as the golden age of Idlewood, when Virginia Maines brought home stories and treasures from her travels, or she could go further and tell them all about how those glory days shattered apart with one horrendous deed—

But no. First, those stories weren't proven: All Emily had were theories and a few passing mentions in an old document her parents had dismissed as "not enough." Second, these kids didn't want the whole tale. Charlie was a math guy, and as for Anna . . . kids like her weren't interested in history. She was just bored and looking for conversation. And sure, the true tale of adventure and scandal and fallen heroes was interesting, more interesting than Roman key rings, but if she raised that story, then what? If they knew everything, they'd turn the history into nothing more than a treasure hunt, and she didn't want that for Idlewood.

"Idlewood was built in 1885 by the Gardner family," Emily finally said. "They lived here until 1929, when they moved to South Carolina."

"And that's when Elaine made the house a hotel," Anna said.

Emily frowned at the very familiar use of Mrs. Gardner's name. "Yes, Mrs. Gardner did," she said.

"Why'd she do that?"

Oh, Emily had *theories*. But instead she said, "Who knows? Maybe the Gardners just wanted to live somewhere closer to civilization. People move. But some think Mrs. Gardner saw a chance to help out the community. She hired local people to run the place once the guests started to arrive."

"What did the house look like before the renovation?" Charlie asked.

Emily waved her hands. "Like this. Mrs. Gardner was adamant that the house stay just as it was, except for some small alterations."

Charlie raised his eyebrows. "So the numbers on the doors were there before?"

Both girls stared at him. "Added later," Emily said. "When it became a hotel. They've probably been updated since then, though, to keep them nice and shiny."

"Hmm," Charlie said.

"What?"

"Oh. Nothing. Just wondering who oversaw the renovations."

Emily had been wondering a little about the renovations herself. The house's second floor had been closed until this weekend. It made sense that Mr. Llewellyn would fix it up. But he said he'd changed things. Small things, yes, but what if he altered something that made this house inauthentic in some way?

That only meant Emily had to work harder.

"The renovations? Probably the Gardners, to some extent," she said, pulling herself from her worries to answer Charlie's question. "But they would have needed workers to supervise the work on the ground. I bet there are books about Idlewood's history in the library."

"Thanks. I saw the library today. I definitely want to explore it some more."

Anna laughed. "And I've been wondering how long it would take for you to go there. Not long, I guess."

Emily turned to Anna. "What's your interest in the house?"

Anna met Emily's eyes, and her gaze hardened. For a moment Emily saw, again, the girl who'd unapologetically gone into the airplane room without asking. "Just interested in the place I'm staying at," she said. "I keep feeling like there's more to Idlewood than meets the eye."

A cold chill went down Emily's back. Anna sounded like she knew something, but if she did, why was she asking? Did she, like Emily, have another reason for coming to Idlewood? Or was she just some bored kid who'd stumbled into evidence of the Shaughnessys' theories?

Either way, this girl was dangerous. Reckless, fearless, dangerous. If Emily had harbored any desire to reveal her theories about Idlewood, Anna would take that tiny bit of knowledge and start knocking down doors. She'd trample any historic evidence Emily needed and ruin Idlewood, all on her own.

Anna tilted her head. "So, Emily, what do you know about Virginia Maines?"

That name! Emily stood up, grabbing her plate at the last moment to keep it from spilling all over the carpet. "Can't help you there. I'm not into Indiana Jones–type history," she said. "I'd better go do some homework before bed."

She hurried off. That was *way* too close. She'd have to keep an eye on Anna. Idlewood itself was counting on her.

Emily strode into the entry hall and froze.

The bald man from the Arctic Circle room was standing over the dragon statue that Emily had moved across the room. His hand was on its head, and he was bent over it almost protectively.

Emily hurried past, causing him to glance up at her with a quizzical expression on his face. She'd hidden her bag with its camera and all its interesting pictures and notes in the library after leaving Charlie in her family's suite, so she went there to claim it before bed. Her bag was on the third shelf from the left, tucked high between two stacks of Agatha Christie novels, first editions. She'd climbed on an old armchair and grabbed it when she heard a knock.

She glanced back at the door, but no one was there. No, the knocking was coming from inside the room. Still up on the chair, Emily scanned the library.

There. Through a few gaps in the shelves, she could see a man, suitcase stuck full of travel pins, wearing a stethoscope and tapping at the wall. One knock, then a step forward, then another two knocks. Searching.

Emily lowered herself off the chair as quietly as she could and tiptoed out of the library. Once out the door, she started running.

The bald man was gone when she reached the entry hall, but there was a short woman, probably one of the tour group, bent beside the carved door, peering at the locks. Emily's eyes narrowed. Anna, the bald man, Suitcase Man, the short woman . . . it had not been easy for the Shaughnessys to get a reservation at Idlewood. They'd had to fight for it, and they did because they had a better reason than just "we need a vacation."

It hadn't occurred to Emily that the other guests might have motivations that were just as strong.

Ten rooms. Ten groups. How many of them had come for their own secret reasons? The treasure of Virginia Maines, if real, was a powerful draw.

But searching for that treasure the wrong way could damage an old and important house. Emily hurried to the Rome suite. Her parents needed to know what she'd seen. They'd know what to do.

"Mom! Dad!" she said as she came back into the room.

No answer. Her parents must still be at dinner, or going to see the pianist Mr. Llewellyn had brought in to play a selection of old music. Or maybe they were out collecting proof that Idlewood was a living photograph of the past.

Should she go get them? No. Here, alone in her family's suite, Emily was sure she was overreacting. So what if Anna and Mr. Llewellyn and Suitcase Man and Short Lady and all the rest of the guests and even the rest of the *world* was against her? (Not that she knew they were.) Were they looking for treasure? Did they want to solve the mysteries of Idlewood? That was just fine.

Because come hell or high water, Emily Shaughnessy would do it first. She was better prepared than any of them. She'd been the one wandering the halls, documenting every room like the historian she was. If there was a clue in the house, she already had a picture of it.

Virginia Maines. Why had Anna mentioned *that* name?

Never mind. If Anna knew something, there was no time to lose. Emily pulled out her history book and the stacks of Polaroids she'd taken throughout the day and got to work.

8

SATURDAY MORNING dawned clear and pretty, and Charlie's parents had remembered their idea about taking a prebreakfast hike on the Appalachian Trail. "It's the perfect thing to wake up our appetites," his dad said.

Charlie's appetite wasn't the only thing that needed waking. He'd gone to the library after dinner and stayed up late, searching for anything he could on the building and renovation of Idlewood. Emily had been right. The house had been built in the late 1800s, renovated for hotel use in the late 1920s, and Elaine Gardner oversaw the renovation, demanding that the house remain unchanged. Charlie assumed she wanted the house to be the same in case she ever got to live in it again. The man in charge of the day-to-day construction was named Silas Silver.

Could Silver have been the one to nail the original numbers on the doors and leave the clues in the Roman suite? It would be easy for him to do so, a few strokes of paint here, an order to rearrange numbers there. What was he trying to tell Charlie?

Charlie yawned as he followed his parents out onto the grounds. The pond had a thin layer of mist hanging over it, and the sun cut through it in strips. Pretty, but come on! It wasn't helping him solve the puzzle.

He'd worked all night—or it felt that way—searching for the code word that would unlock the Caesar cipher. "Idlewood" didn't work, nor did "Gardner," "Elaine," "Everett," "Silver," or any other name he could connect to the house.

This morning, he couldn't stop thinking about those names, even though they were wrong. They kept circling in his brain.

Maybe it was good to get out of Idlewood. A walk would refresh his mind.

It wasn't a long walk to the forest trail. A few other guests were out enjoying the morning. Braid Lady, now with her hair in a messy bun, was reading a book titled *Monkeys, Mobsters, and More* near the flower beds, and the man from the Sunglasses Couple was standing beside the tower, cradling something in his arms. When the man saw the Hendersons, he jolted and quickly stepped out of sight.

Charlie frowned. What was that about?

"Hurry up!" Anna called, and Charlie raced to join his family, who had pulled ahead.

As they hiked, Charlie had to smile. The only reason

Anna wasn't leading the pack was because she kept zig-zagging across the trail, climbing rocks, examining trees, and glancing back at Idlewood with a distant look on her face. Like a bee buzzing from flower to flower or a pirate searching for treasure.

If Charlie had that kind of restless energy, maybe he would have figured out the code by now. Or figured out why the code mattered.

"Anna, get down from there!" his mom called about twenty minutes into the hike. "You're going to get poison ivy."

Anna, who had been using a thick vine to climb an old, gnarled tree, jumped down, grinning. "Any poison ivy that grew here has been dead for a long time."

"That just means the vine is old and brittle," their mom said. "Can't you just stay on the path?"

"What fun would that be?" Charlie muttered. Anna flashed a smile in his direction as the Hendersons kept walking.

As their parents forged ahead, Anna dropped back to walk beside Charlie. "What was that?" she said, cupping an ear. "Am I right in assuming that you might be willing to climb the next one with me?"

Charlie's stomach lurched just imagining it. "Um, not today."

"Oh." Anna's face fell.

She wants me to. Really? Why? Charlie tried to pick at the problem that was Anna. "Maybe someday," he said. "But . . . I kind of want to just enjoy the weekend."

"Okay." Anna jumped off the path to climb a rock.

Their parents stopped once they realized their kids had fallen behind. Charlie's dad's shoulders slumped as he saw his daughter perched on top of a rock. "Honey, I know Idlewood isn't your dream vacation, but the longer we're out here, the longer before we can eat breakfast."

"Sounds like you managed to wake up your appetite," Charlie said. He eyed the rock. It wasn't *that* high.

"Yes, and I'd like to put it to sleep again." His dad grimaced. "They have *omelets*, Anna! We can escape the house again later, but can we get a move on now?"

Anna shrugged, up there on her rock. "You go ahead. I just want a few minutes here."

Charlie's parents looked at each other, probably considering all the other times they'd left Anna unattended and something bad happened, going all the way back to Charlie's first birthday, when they found Anna chin-deep in a bowl of blue icing, wearing half of it as well as a big grin.

But now Charlie was surprised to see Anna gazing at Idlewood with a dreamy frown. *She won't cause trouble this time*, he thought. *There's more going on than meets the eye.*

So he did the only thing he could think to do: squeeze his lips together and clamber up on the rock with Anna. "I'd like a few minutes, too," he said. "It's nice out here."

"Okay, if you're sure," his mom said, and when Charlie nodded, their parents turned and went back to the house.

Charlie glanced down. Whoa. The rock hadn't seemed so high from down there. He turned his attention to counting the shiny flecks of mica in the stone.

"You didn't have to do that," Anna said.

Charlie risked a look at his sister. She was digging a stick into a crack in the rock.

"I wanted to," he said.

"Really?"

"Yeah." He patted the stone. "It's a good rock. I wonder how long it's been here." Maybe his mysterious codemaker had come out here for lunch. It would be a good private place to plan a cipher, away from the house, surrounded by trees.

Thinking about that kept him from focusing on how high up he was.

Anna smiled. "I know! Imagine who else might have climbed this rock. She probably came here all the time."

She? Mrs. Gardner? Was she the one to set the clue in the doors, if it wasn't Mr. Silver? "We should bring Emily out here," Charlie said. "She knows a lot about the house."

And with that, Anna's smile vanished. "Oh. Emily. How did you meet her, again?"

"I went to see the Rome suite," Charlie explained. "Her family is staying there, so she let me in. It was pretty easy."

"Right," Anna said. "I should have asked permission. I know. You don't have to tell me."

"I wasn't," Charlie started. He'd thought he was doing

so well, but then he had to go and mention Emily. That seemed to be when things went wrong.

But it was fine. He could fix it.

Charlie opened his mouth to tell Anna about the code he'd found, but he stopped himself. Talking about codes wouldn't fix whatever he'd put between Anna and himself—she'd think puzzling over numbers was dorky. But she liked climbing rocks and exploring rooms. So maybe talk about that?

"I wish I'd gone with you," he said, feeling the awkward shape of the lie in his mouth. "To see the rooms. I bet they were pretty amazing."

Or maybe it wasn't a lie. Charlie was glad he hadn't gotten into trouble, but he *did* want to see the rooms. Maybe the key to the code was in one of them.

"Yeah, they were," Anna said. "Rosie and Xavier have one with the northern lights painted on the ceiling, and then there was one designed to look like the inside of an airplane."

"Sounds cool. Cool, but really . . . gray."

Anna shrugged, sliding a foot off the edge of the rock. "Not entirely. There were windows painted with blue outside, and the border around the baseboards had a bunch of red dragons on it."

She fell still, then a smile grew across her face. Anna laughed, jumping off the rock. "*Now* I get it," she whispered when she landed, just loud enough for Charlie to hear it.

"What?" Charlie turned and slowly slid down the

rock, feetfirst. He fell the last few inches and stumbled over to Anna. "What do you get?"

For a moment, Anna didn't answer. She looked up at Idlewood, at the tower jutting up from its corner. Then she looked at Charlie. "The airplane," she said, hushed, like she was revealing a big secret. "Virginia Maines's airplane was called the *Dragon*."

"Oh." For a moment, Charlie had wondered if somehow Anna had found the code word all on her own. But no. This was just another connection to the explorer she loved so much. At least she was having a good time, but it wasn't exactly helping Charlie solve his puzzle.

Or maybe . . . there were those big dragon statues in the entry hall. And one of them had been moved! The airplane room baseboard was painted with dragons, and the China suite had dragons in statue and painted form. Could it be that the clue wasn't hidden in the history of Idlewood but in its decorations?

Charlie started bouncing. "I have to go," he said, and he ran back toward Idlewood. By the time he'd reached the house, he had slowed to a walk and was wheezing.

Anna hadn't followed him. As far as Charlie knew, she was still out in the woods, turning over rotten logs and climbing anything that could be climbed. His parents wouldn't like that, but Anna was the older sibling. She could take care of herself. Probably.

And Charlie had a theory to test. He speed-walked inside and stopped beside the twin dragon statues. Grinning, he patted their heads like a couple of good dogs.

Then he went upstairs to retrieve his notebook and bring it down to breakfast. The omelets smelled delicious, and his appetite had awakened as well.

He filled a plate and found a seat in the far corner of the room, away from his parents, Emily's parents (though Emily herself was absent), Rosie and Xavier, and anyone else. And there, using the code word *dragon*, he unlocked the Caesar cipher.

THEY ARE SAFE
TREASURE ISLAND

◆ ◆ ◆

Emily didn't have time for breakfast. She had too many mysteries to solve and not enough time to solve them. So while her parents went downstairs, Emily stayed in bed, hair uncombed, still in pajamas, sorting through the history of Idlewood.

She wasn't sure what she was looking for. Something that didn't belong to Elaine and Everett Gardner, something that stood out as different, either in the books or the pictures. Something changed, but long ago. Something that could tie the Gardners, Idlewood, and Virginia Maines together in a nice, neat friendship bracelet for Emily.

Had Virginia lived here? Emily had a letter that said so, but that wasn't proof on its own.

So Emily scoured the pictures, trying to find the details her parents seemed to always see. First the dining room. Then the library. That interesting indoor green-house with all the exotic plants. Where was the clue she was looking for?

Emily laughed and pushed her hair back. The clue? She was talking like a conspiracy theorist or treasure hunter! She wasn't after some pot of gold at the end of Virginia Maines's rainbow; she was here to end the lies and preserve history. So . . . evidence, maybe? Artifacts?

Goodness knew Idlewood had enough of them. Emily spread out her pictures, arranging them room by room. Vases, statues, tapestries made of everything from cloth to woven grasses . . . to say nothing of the porce-lain plates and shiny silverware. But those were just trap-pings, some left there after the house became a hotel, if the old black-and-white pictures in Emily's parents' book were anything to go by.

Emily eyed the book, examining a picture of the ball-room in which the fluffy armchairs facing the paintings were notably missing. Not that those mattered—they came with the hotel renovations. She needed something from *then*, from the night everything went wrong, like the books in the library, maybe, or the paintings—

The paintings. *The paintings*. Emily scrambled to her knees, swirling the bedsheets and causing Polaroids to flutter to the ground. She snatched up a few before they fell, the ones she had taken of the paintings of the Gardner family, and set them next to the old pictures in the book.

They were old, they were grainy, but there was no mistake: The paintings had been *different* in the 1920s.

Emily was sure of it. In the original of one painting of Mrs. Gardner, her arm hung straight. Now, it was bent and seemed to be carrying something. Changing the layout of the furniture was one thing, but why change the paintings?

It was a sign. Evidence. Dare she say . . . a clue.

And she had been the one to find it.

Blood racing, Emily closed the book on the Polaroids of the ballroom and scooped it up. Barefoot, still in pajamas, she charged downstairs. She had to see the paintings for herself and know what the Gardners were trying to tell her.

She ran so fast that she barely registered the fact that one of the dragon statues—in fact, the one she'd moved—was missing.

9

NORMALLY, a morning hike would have made Anna's day, and to tell the truth, it almost did. The forest was beautiful, but more importantly, it held so much stuff to do. It was where she had found the key, after all! If it hadn't been for her parents pushing her to stay on the path and keep walking, it would have been paradise.

Or if Charlie hadn't been assigned to babysit her. Again. Anna frowned over her cold omelet. She'd stayed out in the forest long after Charlie had run off like something bit him, letting him be the one to explain to their parents why she was left unattended.

Not that Charlie could do anything wrong in their parents' eyes.

Still, Anna thought, chewing on a bit of tomato, Charlie *had* climbed the rock with her that morning. That was unexpected. But nice. Almost like the way it used to be, when they were little. Maybe Charlie hadn't completely lost his sense of adventure.

Then Anna remembered him huddling on the rock like it was some sheer cliff and grimaced. All that fear, and it wasn't like the rock was some big risk. It was no secret that Anna understood risks, and she understood them better than Charlie and her parents thought she did. Despite their opinions, Anna didn't take unnecessary risks. Just necessary ones.

Speaking of which, there was a tower room calling her name. Anna turned in her plate and wasted no time going to the bookcase door. Grinning, she yanked on its shelves.

They didn't budge.

"What?" Anna pulled harder, but the door stayed firmly closed.

"Open. You. Big. Stupid. Thing!" she grunted, tugging over and over. Exhausted, she said, barely holding back a shout, "I know you can. I saw it!"

But the fact remained that the door was now securely sealed.

Groaning, Anna sat against the wall and wiped her forehead. What now?

She couldn't stay here. What if Mr. Llewellyn or someone saw her messing with the bookcase? Given her history, they wouldn't take it well. So she stood up, threw a glare at the bookcase, and left.

What to do? She could stay in the main house today, or go out to the forest again. It was shaping up to be a nice, warm day. The forest would be pleasant and full of adventure. And the wooden roof she'd seen from the tower tickled her mind. She wanted to find the building it belonged to. Yes, that would be a good plan. She passed Charlie rummaging through the library and shot an innocent smile at Mr. Llewellyn, who was talking with Emily's parents in the entry hall.

However, as soon as Anna stepped into the warm sunlight, she wished she was feeling it through the dirty glass of a dusty window in the tower. They had forests at home, but Idlewood was special. Idlewood had been the home of Virginia Maines, extraordinary explorer! She *had* to get back up into that tower.

How? The door was sealed.

Anna circled the house to face the tower. Virginia wouldn't have let a little thing like a locked door keep her out of a place she wanted to explore. This was a woman who built her own raft to sail the islands in the Pacific, storms or no storms, and came back with more supplies than she set out with! She had a secret entrance to her tower, for crying out loud.

And Anna suspected that a woman who had one secret entrance to her room might have another. If she was right, she may have found it already.

There were the raised stones on the outside of the tower, the ones Anna had climbed before. Smooth, like they were made for climbing. They probably were.

Anna pulled herself up to the ledge, just like before. From there, she looked up to a line of jutting stones reaching up to the roof.

She glanced around quickly. This would be a long climb, and she didn't need anyone tattling on her. No one was on the lawn, so Book Lady with her latest read and the Sunglasses Couple must have gone inside. She wiped the moisture off her hands and started to climb.

It was easy! Virginia had definitely made this wall to be climbed. How much had she been involved with its construction? Maybe new letters would tell Anna everything she wanted to know, if she could find them.

She pulled herself up on the roof. The wind was cool, and sunlight rippled on the pond. Some of the older guests, especially the lady tourists, were sunning by the water. Down below, on the other side of the house, the family with all the little kids (today, wearing neon-blue shirts, though Anna couldn't tell if they had a slogan on them) played tag beside the maze. One of them stopped and looked up. He pointed at Anna.

Ducking, Anna crawled away. She searched the tower, looking for another way in. What if Virginia had built the steps only to get to the roof? Maybe she liked to take her tea up here or something.

Anna looked over the edge and swallowed. Normally she wasn't scared of heights, like Charlie was, but that was a long drop. It would be hard to climb down. But once she got inside, she'd be okay. She could just take the stairs down. Surely the door would unlock from the inside.

If she could get into the tower.

A moment later, Anna found the next row of climbing

stones. They were right under the window, where any intelligent person would guess they'd be. Feeling silly, Anna climbed up to the window. She sat on its sill and fumbled with the clasp. Thank goodness Virginia had been the type to know the importance of a window with clasps on either side!

At first it didn't move, but with some pushing, Anna was able to overcome the years of rust and dirt and force the window up.

She slid inside, sending up clouds of dust.

"Hello, Virginia," she said, grinning. "I'm back. And guess what? I have all day."

◆ ◆ ◆

There were many interesting things about the Idlewood library, Charlie decided. The sheer number of books crammed into the little room was one strange thing. Most old libraries he saw were much better organized.

Another odd thing was the podium left totally empty in the middle of the room. Hadn't there been a book there earlier?

But the oddest thing, to Charlie, was that although the library had everything by Sir Arthur Conan Doyle and much of Agatha Christie, and even books on code-breaking and the history of Rome (a book Charlie rifled through, looking for more hidden clues), it did not seem to be in possession of a single copy of *Treasure Island*.

He spent the whole morning searching book by book, title by title. He scanned the shelves so many times his eyes ached, and he ran his hands over the spines for so long his fingertips stung.

Sucking on his fingers and worrying slightly about what effect the old germs on the books might have on his body, Charlie sank into a crouch beneath a large window. "Where is it?" he moaned.

It *had* to be here. The code's solution was *They are safe / Treasure / Island*. Why put that book's title in a code unless it meant something?

Standing, Charlie went to look for the records about Idlewood. He needed to know more about the house. What was the significance of the book he was looking for?

Silver? The name of the overseer and also the name of the pirate in *Treasure Island*? Could that be the connection? The book title could have been a sign-off, a code name from the sender. Made sense if it was Silver. But the title was separated from the message, and it had even been broken in two, with the codes for "TREASURE" and "ISLAND" appearing separately in the mural.

The record book Charlie found was basically a coffee-table book about how the house went from being residential to being a hotel. There were pictures of before and after, though they were so grainy and old that Charlie didn't see how any of them could be helpful. He needed a story.

So he read. He read on and on about Mr. Gardner's courtship of his wife, Elaine. He read about their three

119

children and their peaceful lives at Idlewood. And he read about the way they suddenly left the house they had loved, turning it over to the town as a fancy hotel.

And Elaine demanded it be left as it was. Loose threads of a puzzle teased at him. Why leave it at all, if they loved it enough to want it unchanged, if they hoped to come back one day? What had happened?

Or had they left it unchanged? Hmm. Maybe he should check those pictures again. If he saw a change, then maybe *that* would be the clue he needed. Or perhaps he needed to research more, find another book, spend more time searching for the background he needed to solve this puzzle.

Charlie checked the time. He'd been reading for an hour. Smiling, he tried to imagine Anna sitting quietly and reading a dusty book for so long. No, she'd be out *doing* something instead of hanging around here.

And he should be, too. Charlie left the library, carrying the record book with him. If this was a treasure hunt, like in *Treasure Island*, then he shouldn't leave the map behind. He'd return it when he was done with it.

"But please don't lead me into someone's bedroom," he muttered to the book.

The entry hall echoed with Charlie's footsteps. From the parlor, he could hear Book Lady and Suitcase Man bickering over something, though he couldn't make out what they were saying. From the dining room, a busy conversation was going on between Rosie and Xavier and a few of the older guests. Emily's parents were leaning over a little table, muttering excitedly over a crystal clock.

Idlewood was full, but Charlie suspected it wouldn't be for long; it was a beautiful morning, and soon everyone would head outdoors, like the T-Shirts family had. He could hear the joyful shrieks of the younger kids running around outside. That was probably where Anna was—out exploring the grounds. He hoped she didn't do something stupid.

He had wanted to spend time with her this vacation. But she was always missing, and besides, he couldn't keep the code out of his mind.

Taking the book, Charlie traveled to each room, turning the pages to the pictures of the rooms as they had been when the Gardners lived there. He went back to the library first, since it was empty. It looked the same, so the clue he was looking for wasn't here.

The parlor was filled not with Suitcase Man and Book Lady but with an older couple by the time Charlie arrived. The wife, a gray-haired lady who had been examining the furniture, asked him about his morning, while the husband, a man with a huge mustache, asked where Anna was. After just shrugging as his answer, he noted that the parlor was the same, and the dining room also seemed the same, down to the little table outside with its menu for the day's meals. Rosie was there, eating a slice of apple pie. She smiled at Charlie as he passed through. "Hello," she said. "What are you up to?"

"Exploring," Charlie said, tucking the book away.

Rosie nodded. "Just like your sister."

"Have you seen her anywhere?"

Rosie shook her head. "I'm sure she's fine. Probably just looking for ghosts or something. That's what I would have done when I was her age."

The skin at the back of Charlie's neck grew cold. "Ghosts?"

The woman chuckled. "It's an old house. Who knows what's happened here?" She wiggled her fingers and smiled. "You know, I still haven't been able to to see your family's suite. Any chance you could get your parents to give me a tour?"

"Um, sure," Charlie said, and then he left, happy to escape. Not that he believed in ghosts. They were . . . totally irrational. Still, in the old, empty house, with its secret, irrational codes, it was easy to feel every draft of air like a pair of ghostly hands on his skin.

Emily's parents were wandering the entry hall. When they saw Charlie, the father waved, and then both adults went into the parlor. Charlie heard them greet the Gray Hair and Mustache couple.

What *had* that woman been doing when Charlie had seen her before, kneeling down to look under a sofa? Probably nothing. Probably dropped a piece of candy.

The indoor greenhouse was wildly different from the pictures in the book, but that didn't seem too odd. In the book, the garden was neatly kept, which made sense if Everett was a gardener himself. After time, it would become a bit wilder, the way Charlie saw it now. As for the ballroom, it seemed pretty much the same: wide-open floor, paintings around the sides.

The armchairs were different, though. Charlie sat in one, but as he did, he realized it was probably a change made to accommodate all the people who would be staying in a hotel. They couldn't all loiter in the parlor.

A snap, like a book slamming closed, echoed in the room, and Charlie stood up. Someone else was here with him. He glanced around until he spotted Emily, in front of the paintings on the other side of the room. She had her math book tucked against her chest and was darting out of the ballroom in a fast walk just shy of a run.

Charlie closed his book. Not loudly, but the little sound there echoed, and Emily stopped and faced him.

"Oh, Charlie," she said. "What are you doing here?"

"I'm sorry. I didn't mean to scare you," he said.

"You didn't. I just . . . I didn't hear you come in."

Was she in her pajamas? It was almost lunchtime. *She's distracted*, he thought. But why?

"You were busy." Charlie walked over to her. "The pictures are nice. How long have they been here—do you know?"

"The paintings? Yeah. I guess they're okay. I have to go," Emily said. "You caught me at a bad time. I have a lot of important . . . stuff I need to do. I need to get dressed, and I haven't eaten yet. See you later."

Emily ran out of the room.

"Bye," Charlie said. *Guess they're okay?* Charlie would

have thought she'd have a lot more to say about those old paintings! She might also have known things about Idlewood that could have helped him. But it looked like this code was his alone to break.

Charlie opened his book to a random page. Where to next? He looked down at the pages.

A floor plan. That was helpful. He could see rooms he hadn't checked yet. There was the first floor, taken care of. And all the suites on the second floor.

Charlie swallowed. Would he really have to poke around those rooms? And what about those other second-floor rooms on the map, past the hallway with the suites?

Huh. Charlie hadn't known there were rooms that way. He hadn't thought to explore the house's every corner (though he was sure Anna had). And even more interesting was the hallway itself—how it seemed to lead to nowhere.

He traced the upstairs hallway with his finger. Yep. It just ended. Now why would it do that?

Cradling the book, Charlie hurried to the second floor. He passed all the guests' suites and turned onto the next hallway. These doors weren't numbered, and although the hall was clean, it had the air of not being lived in for a long time.

And there, at the end of the hall, was a bookcase. Grinning, Charlie quickened his walk to a run.

He got there so quickly that he almost slammed into the shelf. It wasn't very full, only one stack of books beside a grimy fake plant. But if one of those books was—

"Yes!" He picked up the book on the top of the stack. *Treasure Island*. If Charlie had wanted to hide a book, he would have done it in a library, not in an empty hallway. But then again, that was the first place he'd checked. Silver or Elaine or Mr. Gardner, whoever it was, had planned this clue well!

The bookcase shook. Charlie leaped back, dropping the book on the carpet. He eyed the shelf, breathing heavily, but it didn't happen again.

What the heck? Charlie took a deep breath and scooped up the book. He hadn't imagined it, had he? The shelf had really shaken?

If it had, there was no sign of the tremor. The cheap plastic plant hadn't fallen over or anything. But Rosie's comment about ghosts came back to him. Idlewood was an old house, after all. Could there be dark stories in its history that no one knew about? Ones that could have created a ghost?

Holding the book between white fingers, he turned and fled down the hall. As he passed the Serengeti suite, an unearthly howl from inside cut through the air. Charlie gasped, choking on his own breath, and sped past faster, not stopping until he was back in the quiet library.

He sat in his now-favorite brocade armchair, gulping for air. What had he seen? What had he heard?

Safe and surrounded by books, Charlie returned to logical thought. Probably just an illusion. He must have bumped the bookcase, and its resulting wobble startled him. And the howl? Just someone watching TV.

But this house didn't have any TVs.

Charlie shuddered, then dismissed the thought. Anna would never be scared by something so silly. He turned *Treasure Island* over in his lap. Here it was. Now, where was the clue?

Again, was the code related to Silver? Or to this book? Now that Charlie had found a copy, hidden somewhere out of the way, he had a hard time believing it was coincidence. No, this book was meant to be found, but only by someone who knew what they were looking for. So what was he looking for?

Charlie searched the book from cover to cover. No papers hidden in the pages, and neither front nor back covers seemed too thick, like they were hiding a paper in the binding. No writing on the pages or circled letters.

Circled letters. Wait. There was more than one way to put a code in a book. Maybe this was a *book code.*

That made a lot of sense. For a book code, the person encoding the message would use the words inside a book, marking their location with a string of three numbers. The numbers could indicate a page number, then a specific line on that page, and word in that line. For example, 53-12-7 would point to the fifty-third page, the twelfth line on that page, and the seventh word in that line. But that only worked with a specific edition of a book. Sure, that made a book code extra hard to break because it required both the sender and the receiver to have the same exact edition, but it also made the code nearly impossible to solve if it was difficult to find two copies of the same edition, or if a book had many editions and reprints.

Like *Treasure Island.*

But since the mural didn't specify an exact edition, that could mean Charlie was dealing with a *different* form of a book code, one that was less secure but more flexible. In this kind of code, the numbers would correspond to the chapter number, the specific paragraph in that chapter, and then the specific word in that paragraph. The code would be a list of word locations that would be true of any edition, and the receiver could, in their own copy of the book, look up each word until it created a message.

Charlie pushed his glasses up his nose, hand shaking not with terror over imagined ghosts (he was sure they were imagined) but with excitement. Another thing about book codes was that they were perfect for longer messages.

Was this it? The final message, the real reason why the clues had been set in doors and walls? Charlie hoped it was, and that all he'd have to do was solve this book code and uncover it all!

But his energy faded as quickly as it came. So what if he'd found *Treasure Island*? It was only the means to read a code. The code itself was still out there, hidden.

Where? Was the clue hidden in one of the codes he'd already solved, or would he have to search for it?

Charlie's stomach growled. Outside the library, people were filing into the dining room.

Lunchtime.

It was no good thinking on an empty stomach. He'd solve it later. One way or another, he'd find the message he needed and solve the book code.

Charlie left the library, book tucked under his arm. As he passed through the hall, he frowned. Where had the crystal clock on the table beside the dining room gone?

10

THE TOWER ROOM was surprisingly cozy, once Anna got past all the dust. A perfect place to work.

First she dug through the drawer she'd found earlier with the compass, picture, and letter. Maybe she'd missed something. Anna set the compass down on the desk and placed the picture frame with the two sisters right beside it. "Hey, Ginny," she said, touching the old photo. "I found your other staircase."

Holy cow, she had really lived here! Here, in Idlewood! And to think, this whole room had been hidden away for decades. No one had ever seen it before, except for Virginia and the Gardners—and now, Anna herself.

It was like hearing distant thunder, to think about it. And it filled Anna with lightning. She jumped up and started the hunt.

Two letters lay beside Virginia's bed. In a stack of charts on the highest platform, Anna found another.

Three more on the next platform, poking out from under a stack of charts beside the dresser! And finally, sandwiched between old papers covered in numbers (Longitudes? Latitudes? A travel budget?), Anna found one more letter.

It seemed fitting that Virginia's records would require a treasure hunt to find them. There was a story, not well documented, about Virginia being asked to investigate some Mayan ruins. She had agreed, and come out of the ruins with jewelry and stones carved with ancient stories, which she'd handed over to the authorities (who had reportedly gifted her with some jewelry of her own). Perhaps she had been the first in centuries to see those carvings.

Just like Anna was the first person to see these letters in many years. Maybe there were stories in them that no one else knew about. Adventures even grander than the ones in all the books Anna had read about Virginia Maines. She'd be the first, after so long, to know.

Anna took the letters back to the desk and carefully set them down in a stack. She didn't want to harm the old paper if she could help it, especially not when she knew who these letters belonged to. She found the oldest (one from beside the dresser) and began to read.

Dear Ginny,
Your stories of the people you met on your journeys in the Pacific Islands were swell! I suppose children are the same no matter where

you are. I admit, I have been thinking about children quite a bit lately. After all, soon you will be an aunt!

Anna pulled back from the letter, smiling. She could imagine Virginia, away in some foreign locale, jumping up and down with the joy that Elaine was going to have kids.

We have been using the tea set you brought us. Everett in particular loves it, though he suggests we only use it for special occasions. I disagree; I love it too much, and we have had so few special occasions lately! I will have to use it when Everett is at work, as he often is.

I'm sure you won't mind, but I shared your last letter with Everett. He was charmed by your sketches of the stilt houses of the Caroline Islands and asked me to ask if you wouldn't prefer a house rather higher in the air, perhaps in the branches of a tree. He also wants me to add that he hopes you do not break your arm trying to build one on your own.

Yes, I told him about your little misadventure. It serves you right for telling about my embarrassing piano recital at the wedding! And I wouldn't have done it if I didn't know that now we could both laugh about it. I admit, the fault was as much mine as yours. We both loved that book, though with its tales of treasure and adventure on the high seas, perhaps the story of Jim Hawkins and Long John Silver spoke to you more than to me. I know how cheated you felt that Ben Gunn made his home in a cave, not a tree house. You always did like seeing the world, even if it was just from a high place.

Which is why I feel a little sad that we don't have a tree house of our own at Idlewood. Somewhere high above it all. Perhaps one day, we will build one, just you and me, and we can model it after the one you, in your frustration, drew on the cover of <u>Treasure Island</u>, just so the book would have at least one tree house! Although I fear that may have to wait for many years, as I imagine I may have my hands full soon with little ones. But I don't mean to be such a wet blanket. After all, there's still time. When you come back to visit, perhaps we can make a plan for its construction once the children are old enough. Though you will have to do the climbing. The thought of being so far from the ground turns my bones to jelly. And no, no amount of persuasion from you will change my mind! I'm serious!

Speaking of which, I told Everett about your idea for a tower. He said we don't have the money to spend adding a whole section of the house just for you, but he hopes that maybe, soon, that will change. He says you're welcome to stay with us whenever you'd like and if you find any exotic plants, to bring cuttings for him.

Hoping to see you soon,
Elaine

It seemed Elaine shared Charlie's fear of heights. And, Anna thought, touching her arm where her own bone had been broken on that ill-fated pier trip, it seemed she and Virginia had something in common, too.

And yet Elaine and Virginia seemed to be so close, teasing and swapping stories even after one was married, while Anna and Charlie struggled to do anything together.

"Why?" she wondered out loud.

Anna looked at the date on the letter. January 1922. After the wedding but still years before Virginia's disappearance in 1925. What had happened between those dates? She picked up another letter and read it.

Dear Ginny,

Why didn't you tell me that you would be traveling to Greece and Rome on this latest expedition? Perhaps you did tell me. Perhaps I remember that you did, and in fact that you told me often. But if I had fully understood (and had not been troubled by looking after little Simon), I would have traveled with you.

Laugh if you want; I understand that I have shuddered at many of your travels. But Rome is not the canoe trip down the Mississippi you invited me to join you on. In Rome, I would have access to comfort far beyond what a tent could offer. Besides, I have always wanted to go to Rome! It is where great thinkers and writers shared their thoughts with the world! It is where my beloved Caesar cipher was born!

And now I've slain you, I can tell. Go ahead and laugh. I have not even told you how I have been leaving Everett love notes written in our own Caesar cipher, with his name as the key. I think it's more fun if the message unfolds over time. Father was right in assigning us our magical nicknames. I am, and will always be, the Sphinx, with my love of riddles. And you, my fiery, treasure-hunting sister, deserve yours just as much. (On a somewhat related note, I found a brooch at the jeweler's that practically calls you by name!)

Which is the key for your code! Of course I'd have one for you,

*too, you bearcat. Enjoy this Caesar cipher in Rome: Tcdkh ylu nlo
tco Dnoeadk jdsh, dkg nlo toustekb jo wetc yluo ilvoiy mdektekb dkg
fdo ln scoüs. E weü hoom tcoj sdno nlo ylu uktei ylu ootuok.*

    Sincerely,
     Your not-quite-so-angry sister Elaine, and also baby Simon

*P.S. The pearl earrings you gave me for my birthday have gone
missing. I was worried Simon swallowed them, but now I remember I
lent them to you last time you visited. Did they find their way into
your bag by accident?*

Anna smiled. Elaine was more like Charlie than she
had thought! Imagine if he had been the one to find this
letter. He would have gotten right to work deciphering
the code.

Anna, on the other hand, didn't bother. She didn't
know how to begin to solve it, and there were other stories to read.

One by one, she read the letters, wandering around
the tower when sitting still became a pain. They were all
short, with a few other codes here and there penned by
Elaine. Elaine would ask questions about Virginia's travels (though, after reading her hero's nickname so often,
Anna was starting to think of her as "Ginny"), assure her
that no, she still did not want to climb any trees, thank
her for any trinkets Ginny had brought back for the family, and tell about how her growing children were doing
and the books she'd read. It seemed that Elaine was fond

of mysteries, first and foremost, but would read anything she could get her hands on.

So Charlie, it was uncanny.

But all these letters, written years before the disappearance, told Anna nothing about *why* Ginny had vanished. Or why the tower and the whole third floor had been left abandoned. She learned that Ginny would come to live at Idlewood between travels, and that Everett did eventually build a tower for her as a kind of upper-class tree house, complaining the whole time about the expense, and that Ginny helped design it, though there was no word on whether Ginny and Elaine ever got their *real* tree house. She learned about life at Idlewood, as Elaine had another child and got used to being a mother. She even read a letter from Everett, asking Ginny all about her travels and if she could bring back some jade from China for Elaine's birthday and maybe a bonsai tree for himself.

Yet one voice was missing: Ginny's. Reading these letters, Anna could see the background around the adventurer: her sister, her life, her travels. Elaine would say things like, "It sounds like Kiwako is becoming quite a handful to her parents," "Did you tell Brigid that we would buy any quilts she would sell us? I hope you did," and, "For the last time, please pack extra mittens or you know what will happen," making Anna wonder how many stories Ginny and Elaine shared that weren't written here. The scraps and hints were like the paper around a cutout shape, but the shape itself was missing. And Anna really, really wanted to see it.

Once the letters were read, Anna returned to the desk, stacked them neatly, and stuck them in the drawer. Then she looked at the other drawers.

They wouldn't open. Stuck, maybe, clogged by the passage of time or maybe with secret latches! "You would do that, wouldn't you, Ginny?" Anna asked, kneeling in the dust. "I bet it's right under here."

She pried at the bottom of the desk. There was a screw that looked too loose to be a real screw, but it was far back. Maybe if she leaned a little more—

Anna fell face-first. Her collision echoed in the empty room. Coughing, she pushed herself up. No, that wasn't an echo. A worn, scratched, leather-bound book had fallen when she shook the floorboards. It must have been leaning against the desk, standing upright against the wood. Yes—she could see the narrow, clean strip on the ground where the book's bottom edge had kept the dust from covering it, before it fell over.

Oh, this could be so much better than a hidden drawer! Reverently, Anna picked up the book. She hadn't opened it, but she had a hunch about what kind of book this was.

Anna brushed the dust off the book and leaned in to take a deep sniff. The sour smell of old leather and the musty vanilla of paper. And, even after all these years, she thought she could smell the briny scent of the sea.

She cradled the book in her hand and opened it with as much care as she would a mummy's sarcophagus, letting the pages fall open to an entry in the center, where a picture of Ginny posing with a bunch of South Pacific men was stuck between the pages.

Anna pressed her fist against her mouth and let out a scream. It was really Ginny's journal! She moved the picture and read.

> Goodness, one can get lonely on this raft! I can only hope that I don't become so lonely that I start talking to the fish.

Ginny's writing was small, quick, and leaned right, like it was rushing to the end of the sentence. Anna read the story and turned to another one.

> I found a pair of alabaster sphinxes in the market, and I knew I had to buy them. One I'll give to Elaine as a thank-you for the beautiful dragon brooch she gave me, and the other I'll keep for myself.

Anna spent the morning reading story after story.

> The whole world is talking about my brilliance in discovering the secret room in the French abbey. I'm afraid, dear journal, that the truth is rather less brilliant. I stumbled and put my hand into the tapestry and could feel no wall there. Luck is so often on my side, but no one seems to want to give it credit for what I do. So I shall do so here. Let this make up for the brilliance no one saw that one time I found my way to a hidden valley in the Congo.

Hidden valley in the Congo? Anna had never heard that story! She flipped through the pages, searching for the tale, but was sidetracked first by an entry.

> Somehow I am still alive. Though it was a near thing, and I suppose Bradley will kill me later. That wet blanket is always asking me not to take foolish risks. To which I say that no risk I take is foolish.

Anna laughed. "You got that right!"
She read about how Ginny was seeking to cross Brazil on her plane, the *Dragon*. Due to a storm and a mechanical malfunction, the plane's fuel dipped dangerously low. Bradley suggested they lighten the plane. Anna read Ginny's response.

> I hated to lose my plane. And we were so close to our destination! I was sure Bradley was right, that we would have reached it were the <u>Dragon</u> a little lighter. So I endeavored to make it so.
>
> Obviously, I could not have parted with the treasures I'd received. That would be unthinkable! But there was another way. Without asking Bradley's permission, I gave him the controls to the plane. I put on my parachute (you see, I can be wise on occasion!) and tossed myself out before he could stop me. It was a glorious fall. The door was open between the dragon's wings, and I soon grew wings of my own as the green jungle rushed up to meet me. And as you can see, I am

quite all right. I landed with nothing more than a few
bumps and am taking a short break before ankling it
to where Bradley has landed the plane. I will share his
reaction to my stunt in my next entry.

Anna laughed again. She'd never heard the story of
Ginny jumping from the *Dragon*, either. She turned the
page, ready to read about Bradley's response, but then
jumped up. How long had she been up here? Was it
lunchtime?

The grounds looked empty, and she didn't dare risk
running down too late again. The rest of the journal
would have to wait.

Should she bring it with her? No. For now, Anna
wanted Ginny all to herself.

She closed the book, set it on the desk, and started
the climb down the stairs and out through the silent
third-floor hall. There was the door, hidden by the bookcase, at the bottom of the stairs. Anna pushed on it.

It didn't budge.

"What?" Anna whispered. She tried again, and still
it didn't move. She searched for a handle, but there
wasn't one.

COME ON! What kind of sick joke was that, to seal a
door and leave no way to open it from the inside? Anna
could have screamed. Instead, she satisfied herself by
kicking the door, hard, and turning around to stomp
back up to the tower room.

Maybe it's for the best, she thought as she climbed

back out the window. The grounds were empty, after all, which meant the house was not. If she'd gone through the door, maybe she would have run smack into her parents or Mr. Llewellyn. As she climbed back down to earth, the mountain wind blew the dust from her red hair.

◆ ◆ ◆

Emily felt bad about running off on Charlie. But she couldn't hang around. Not when she was on the verge of a huge discovery!

She had raced down to the ballroom, unkempt and still in pajamas, and hadn't been disappointed. Another, closer look revealed that the paintings *had* been changed. Why, Emily wasn't sure. But they had!

A painting of Elaine, once depicting her with one hand on a large dog, now showed her resting that hand on a panda bear, of all things. Also, in a basket hanging from Elaine's other arm, a book was nestled. Squinting at the old picture in her book, Emily thought that might have once been a bottle.

Dog to panda, bottle to book. Odd for one painting, for sure, but there were others.

Emily walked slowly around the room, stopping by each painting. Not all of them had been changed. There was one of the whole family, the three kids and both parents in front of Idlewood, that Emily couldn't find a single difference in.

But others had glaring changes. In one, a rosebush beside Elaine had been replaced with stalks of bamboo.

In another, one of those gold dragon statues from the hall had been painted in later. And in each painting, someone had added a book. Small, discreet, but there.

As Emily walked, she made another discovery. The ballroom was lined with armchairs, but the ones facing the altered paintings couldn't be moved. She sat down in one and tried to push it, to get a better glimpse of the entire wall, and she couldn't. Kneeling beside it, she saw: It and some of the others had been nailed to the floor.

Someone meant for these paintings to be seen, she thought. *But why?*

What was the message here? Who had changed the paintings?

Elaine Gardner, probably. Elaine was fond of puzzles and codes, and hiding clues in paintings would be exactly her cup of Earl Grey. But why? Were these paintings a map to Elaine's sister's exotic trinkets, like what a treasure hunter might think?

Maybe. Emily didn't consider that option long, though. Treasure hunting wasn't history. It focused too much on gold and riches and not enough on understanding what happened. But a woman giving tribute to her world-traveling sister might be—that could be it! The reason Elaine wanted the house unchanged was to leave a message about Virginia.

Emily curled up in an immobile chair and looked up at Elaine with her hand on the panda. Everything she read said that after June 14, 1925, the Gardners never spoke about Virginia again. It had only been through

Emily's own parents' research that *she* knew the connection between Idlewood and Virginia. If Elaine was scandalized enough to never speak of her sister again, why change the paintings? Why order that the house not be changed?

That was what Emily needed to find out. Perhaps Elaine felt bad about what happened? It must have been hard to lose her sister. Maybe this was her quiet way of saying goodbye. But, and this made Emily's heart race, it could be that there was more to the story than even she had guessed. Maybe Elaine was trying to communicate a secret that had been lost to time!

She had to find out what it was! Finding that answer could make Idlewood stand out. It would save the house, and she had just found the first clue! Thrilled, Emily leaped out of the chair and slammed her book closed. There was no time to lose: She had a mystery to solve.

And that was when Charlie showed up. She excused herself as fast as she could but still felt bad about it. Charlie was nice, and she liked the few conversations they'd had at meals, but he was a math guy, not a historian. He spent all his time looking in that notebook he brought, moving numbers around, instead of appreciating Idlewood in its glory.

As she passed through the entry hall, she heard a woman say, from the second floor, "I know why you *really* came here!" Emily slowed, narrowing her eyes as a woman with long hair pulled back in a sloppy bun and a heavy book tucked under one arm stormed down the stairs, followed by the Suitcase Man, dragging his pin-covered monstrosity. What was that about?

Not that it mattered. Emily had a clue that would save the house, and nothing that man or the short woman or anyone could do would stop her.

After getting dressed, she took her book and the pictures down to a late breakfast. Rosie and her husband were in there, talking to an elderly couple, a man with a pair of sunglasses on his head, and Mr. Llewellyn. The gray owner of Idlewood stared at Emily as she came in.

Rosie wasn't quite as rude. "Hello, Emily," she said. "Did you have a nice sleep?"

"Fine," Emily said. "The rooms are very cozy here."

"They are!" The woman smiled and tilted her head at Mr. Llewellyn. "Evan was just telling us about the suites. You like history, don't you? Why don't you join us?"

Mr. Llewellyn paled. "I don't know if that's—"

"No," Emily said, shaking her head. "I have some homework to do." She held up her book. "Maybe later."

Mr. Llewellyn looked visibly relieved. *Why?* Emily wondered. Because she knew he was selling the house? Or another reason?

It didn't matter, not if she saved the house. Emily took a plate of eggs and sausage (cold, but beggars couldn't be choosers), sat at the end of the table, and compared the pictures in the book to the ones she had taken herself.

A panda instead of a dog. A dragon statue added to the scenery. And a book in each altered picture. Why?

"Evan, I've been curious about the suites," Rosie's

husband was saying to Mr. Llewellyn. "There used to be more suites open to guests, but only ten are numbered and themed, right?"

"Yes, that's right."

"Why?" the woman cut in.

"Mrs. Gardner was a big reader," Mr. Llewellyn said. "She especially loved stories about far-off places."

Emily smirked into her orange juice. *Elaine Gardner wasn't the sister with the love of far-off places,* she thought. *Do you know that, old man? Are you lying to your guests? Do you know Virginia lived here, and are you trying to bury that fact?*

"So we have suites like the Arctic Circle," Rosie said. "And there's also India, Rome . . ."

"The Pacific Islands, air travel, Australia, the Amazon, Egypt, China, and the Serengeti," Mr. Llewellyn finished. "All decorated in the style of their theme."

"They sound wonderful," Rosie said. "You know, we haven't had a chance to see the other suites yet. I'm starting to worry that we might not have a chance this trip. We'll have to come back."

Mr. Llewellyn swallowed. "We'd love to see you again," he said.

He may have said more, but Emily wasn't able to focus on his lies. China! Panda, dragon, bamboo . . . all the additions in each painting were symbols of China! And Idlewood had a China-themed suite.

Emily closed her book and took one last bite of food before she stood to leave. Lunchtime wasn't far away, after all, and it wasn't like she had much of an appetite—at least not for *food*.

A faint sound, like a dog's howl, bled through the walls. The man with the sunglasses stood up and left as pounding footsteps from someone running up above echoed in the entry hall. Emily and all the adults jumped as the sound passed by them. Mr. Llewellyn rubbed his forehead. "That girl" was all he said. Then he stood up and left the room.

They all knew who he was referring to. "She's just excited," Rosie said. "How often does a kid get to stay in a house like this?"

"If she's not careful," the elderly man said, speaking up for the first time, "she's going to break something. Maybe she already has. I might be wrong, but I think some of the more breakable vases and ornaments have gone missing."

His wife tsked. "You're thinking of that bed-and-breakfast in Cape May. They had all kinds of break-ables. That's why they didn't allow children to stay there, remember?"

"Cape May?" Rosie asked. "I've heard it's beautiful. When were you there?"

As the grown-ups started a new conversation, Emily left the dining room. She wandered back to the ballroom, book in hand. A good historian checked her facts. Yes, the pictures *had* been changed, and yes, the alterations all seemed to point to China.

Hmm. If she remembered right, Charlie had said his

family was staying in the China suite. That was perfect. He knew her and would let her look around, like she had for him, and she'd get a chance to apologize for running out of the ballroom so fast.

Emily went upstairs and knocked on the door to Charlie's family's suite.

A moment later, Anna opened the door. Her red curls were wet, like she'd just gotten out of the shower. Odd. Emily hadn't taken Anna for the super-cleanly type. "What do you want?" Anna asked, though her voice lacked the rudeness the phrase implied.

"Um," Emily said. If Anna had just been in the shower, then maybe it hadn't been her tearing through the entry hall like the dead were chasing her. "I thought you were . . . is Charlie here?"

Anna shook her head. "I think he's down in the library." She moved to close the door.

Emily grabbed it. "Wait." Anna frowned at her, and she smiled. "I'd really like to see your family's suite."

"Huh?"

"I haven't seen it yet. And Charlie came to see mine, so I think it's only fair."

Anna sighed. "Fine. I have to finish getting ready for lunch, anyway."

"What have you been doing? Swimming in the pond?"

Anna didn't say anything, but she did let Emily in. Emily marveled at the living room area. There was even a little set of bronze dragons just like the ones in the entry hall but smaller!

"It's beautiful," Emily said.

Anna grinned. "If you like that, wait until you see my room. My mom says she wishes it was hers."

"Lucky you."

Anna shrugged. "I would have picked Charlie's. His has a sword." She waved a hand at her riot of wet curls. "I've got to tame this before the humidity gets to it. Look around, but don't break anything."

"Who do you think I am?" But Emily took her hand off an old silk fan she was admiring. Anna rolled her eyes and went into the bathroom.

Okay, she was in the China suite. What clue was she looking for?

A book? Each painting had one. But as she searched each room in the suite, the only books she could find obviously belonged to the family or had been printed much later than anything Elaine Gardner would have left behind.

On top of that, Emily could only search each room once. Anna would think it was weird if she found Emily wandering back and forth in the suite when she was only supposed to be taking a quick look.

The last room Emily visited was clearly Anna's. It didn't have the sword, and it wasn't the master bedroom. And it was lovely. Emily oohed at the ink painting hanging over the bed, causing Anna to poke her head in. "What?"

"That's gorgeous!"

Anna shrugged but smiled. "I'd still prefer the sword," she said, and left.

Emily looked around. All around the walls were eight painted panels. Four on the left and three on the right, and one beside the door. All scenes with bamboo. It was like standing in a garden.

"Beautiful," Emily breathed. And it was. But why had the paintings led her here?

Paintings. Maybe the clue was in another painting. One of the bamboo scenes?

Or all of them? Emily stepped closer to the one on the far right. Bamboo wasn't exactly a book, but in ancient China, sometimes it was used to make paper, so that was close. And bamboo had been in one of the altered pictures.

Emily stared at the painting, feeling time pass. Three bunches of bamboo. Actually, "bunches" was too generous a word; the first two panels only held a single stalk, and the last had three. A strangely sparse picture, considering how much more detailed the other panels around this room seemed to be.

Had she been here too long? She should have stayed behind when Charlie had visited her family's Roman rooms so she could know how long a friendly visit should last—

Hmm. Rome. If Emily wasn't mistaken, didn't those three bamboo stalks in the last panel look like a *V* and then an *I*?

The Roman numeral for six.

Yes! And the first and second were just I, which meant one.

Emily looked at the next one. It had another three

148

bunches. The next panel, the same. That couldn't be chance.

"Anna!" she called. "Do you have a pen I could borrow?"

"Um, I think Charlie might," Anna called back.

Emily ran to the room with the sword and grabbed the first pen she could find. Once back in Anna's room, she realized she should have also asked for paper. She had her book, and the papers inside, but she *really* didn't want to write on them. One was her parents' book, and the other was important historical documents.

No problem! Her wrist would work fine. She set her book on the bed and wrote down the numerals on her skin: I, I, VI. Then she wrote the next panel's numbers below that.

Some were easy, but most were more complicated. She took a moment to realize the fallen stalk in one panel meant an *L* and crossed stalks cut down the middle by the edge of a boulder formed a *C*. But before long, she had circled the room and had all the sets:

I, I, VI
II, III, XXI
VII, I, II
XXV, IX, LVII
I, XVIII, VII
X, I, XIX
VI, XLI, XCI
XIV, XXVIII, LII

The list now stretched almost to her elbow. Eight panels. Twenty-four numbers. One step closer to finding Elaine's message and saving Idlewood.

"Are you still here?" Anna asked from the door. Her hair had been wrestled into a ponytail.

"Just leaving," Emily sang. Handing the pen to Anna, she hurried out of the China suite. She had to get back to her room so she could transcribe the numbers to paper before they rubbed off or got noticed, and she had to figure out what they meant. Idlewood was counting on her.

LUNCHTIME was weird. Anna sat next to Charlie, both of them eating chicken salad sandwiches, but they could have been on opposite sides of the Atlantic Ocean and it would have made little difference.

They sat in silence broken only by chewing and the chatter of the other guests. Anna hadn't seen much of the other guests, as she had been away in the tower room. They seemed nice. The tour group, as always, buzzed in and out, chatting loudly. The young family was there, their blue T-shirts reading GARDNER GARDENERS, and Rosie smiled at her when she came into the dining room. The Sunglasses Couple kept to themselves. The woman's sleeve looked ragged, almost chewed.

Charlie had an old book open on the table next to him and was frowning over it. Probably found the book in the library. It looked kind of familiar, but Anna couldn't place it.

"Is that any good?" Anna asked.

"What?"

"That." Anna pointed to the book with her sandwich. "Is it any good?"

"Careful, you'll get food on it." Charlie snatched up the book and put it in his lap. "It's . . . confusing," he said.

"If it's confusing, why keep reading it?" Anna asked.

He looked up at her with wide eyes, like he'd never considered the idea of *not* finishing a book. "I need to know." He turned away and poked at his sandwich. "I mean, I need to know how it ends."

Anna grinned. Charlie. Such an Elaine. And she was such a Virginia.

The sisters had managed to stay so close. Why couldn't she and Charlie? Maybe Elaine hadn't thought Ginny was stupid and reckless.

"Want to go exploring?" Charlie asked, out of the blue.

"What?"

"You. Me. Go exploring. Let's see if we can find something unusual." His blue eyes blazed. "You've probably seen every corner of this building. You could show me around. And Emily knows a lot about the house. Maybe we could all explore it together."

"Um." It wasn't that Anna was opposed to Emily. The girl wasn't as obnoxious as she had seemed before, or at least she knew how to turn it off. And Anna was both floored and thrilled that Charlie wanted to go poking around the house. But the third floor waited, and she wanted to read more of that journal!

"You do want to, right?" Charlie asked. He nibbled his sandwich, made a face, and pulled out a tomato. He scowled at it. "In a chicken salad sandwich? Why do bad things happen to good people?" He turned back to Anna. "So?"

"I do, it's just . . . I have something I need to do."

Charlie raised his eyebrows, making his glasses slide down his nose. "What?"

"Just something."

"I could come, too," he said, pushing his glasses back into place.

"No!" Even if Charlie was cool with exploring a secret third floor, the bookcase door was sealed, which meant they'd have to climb up outside the tower. Charlie would never do that.

And, if she showed Charlie the third floor, it wouldn't be a secret place anymore. She wanted it to stay that way. Just a little longer.

"Fine! As long as you're not breaking the rules," he said.

"I'm not." That was true—no one had ever forbidden her from visiting the third floor. Admittedly, the tower climb was a bit more of a gray area.

"Maybe Emily will go with me," Charlie said. He threw his sandwich down on the plate.

"Maybe. Or you could go on your own." Emily hadn't reappeared since she'd raced out of the Hendersons' suite.

"I think I will. But if you see Emily, could you tell

her I'm looking for her? I want to ask her if she's seen anything strange."

"Sure." An empty promise, since Anna only planned to see a dusty tower room for the rest of the afternoon.

"Oh, and Anna?"

"What?"

"Do you believe in ghosts?"

The question was so bizarre, coming from Mr. Math and Logic, that Anna chuckled, and Charlie gave her the same expression he'd given that tomato. "Sorry," she said. "I don't know. Maybe. Why?"

"I thought I heard something earlier. Like . . . a ghostly howl."

"A howl?" Anna hadn't heard it, but she'd been high in the tower. Which seemed like a much better place for ghosts than the main house, now that she thought about it.

"Do you think what I heard . . . could be something?"

"A ghost in Idlewood? No. I don't. But sometimes it does feel like . . ."

"What?" Charlie leaned toward her.

How to explain without giving away the third floor and journal? "Like there's more here than just a house," she finished. "Like . . . something is still here and alive. Not a ghost or anything but something else."

"Like history, maybe?"

"Maybe." Anna stood up, her sandwich devoured. "See you later."

Charlie gave a half-hearted wave, already turning

back to his book, and Anna left, feeling like she'd failed a test. Maybe she should have told him about the third floor when he'd asked about ghosts. Charlie was smart; he'd probably guessed that the house held secrets. But his idea of exploring was looking for another book. He didn't understand the need to see what lay beyond what was already known and recorded.

Anna ran back to the China suite to grab a hat. The constant showers were making her hair even more unruly. A book lay on her bed. Hmm. Anna picked it up and turned it over. Emily's math book. She must have left it here when she was looking around.

Anna knew it wasn't polite to flip through someone else's book, but she instinctively opened it before thought could get in the way.

Her eyes widened. "Those are the weirdest math problems I've ever seen."

Tilting the book, she let a couple of folded papers fall to the bed. They looked like copies scanned from a notebook. A journal, maybe? But on the pages beneath the papers were a series of pictures of dragon statues beside a carved door and an old photo of a stone tower Anna was coming to know very well.

A book about Idlewood? Anna peeled the fake paper cover away from the front of the book. *Idlewood: A Brief History*, the title read. Authored by Jerry and Flora Shaughnessy. Huh. Anna put the cover back.

Anna opened the book again, flipping through pages. She had wondered what the house had been like before.

Even though she had the letters and Ginny's journal, knowing the history itself might be useful.

Skimming, she read pretty much what she already knew from Elaine's letters. Elaine and Everett had married and started having children in Idlewood, where they lived the happy lives of the rich and social. Other details, like the architecture of the house, were pretty boring compared to the adventures Ginny wrote about. Anna found herself drifting away from the text, paying more attention to the sound of someone, probably Charlie, back in the suite, walking around the living room. She put the book down and picked up the papers to slide them back where she'd found them when she spotted the name *Virginia* in the copied script.

What? She stopped, unfolding the papers. She read the sentence with Virginia's name in it. Then, she read it again.

Anna's knees felt weak. Sinking into the bed, she turned back and read the sentence a third time. It hadn't changed, although Anna wished it had.

Mother never imagined her own sister could have ever been wrapped up with the Mob, but she was wrong.

The Mob? Guns and crime and concrete shoes? That was impossible—Anna had read all about Virginia Maines. And sure, the woman was a bit of an enigma, but there had been nothing on any of the websites about her being part of the Mob.

What even was this paper? Anna shuffled through the pages to find their start. It was a letter, not a journal page—a letter from Simon Gardner, Elaine's oldest child.

Dear Mr. and Mrs. Shaughnessy,
   I was very surprised to receive
your letter. In all my years,
no one has ever suggested to me
that the reason the Gardners
abandoned Idlewood was due to a
scandal. This doesn't surprise
me; my parents worked hard to
make sure the scandal was
buried, and they rarely spoke
of it again during the short
years they were both alive. I
remember little of what happened
in the days leading up to June
14, 1925, as I was a very small
child at the time. But I asked
my mother about it years later,
and I can tell you the little
that she told me. I'm not
surprised that my sisters had
nothing to tell you. They were
too young when it happened to
even know to ask about it, like
I did.
   The scandal centered around my
aunt, Virginia Maines, who was an
explorer at that time.

Fingers growing cold, Anna kept reading. Simon
Gardner revealed that for years, Virginia was indeed a

rising star in her world. An explorer known for reckless yet ingenious exploits, a plucky woman who didn't take no for an answer. Her legend grew with every journey she made.

As did her treasure collection. Anna already knew that Virginia typically brought home souvenirs from her travels. A number of them were mentioned in the letters. But when the items never made it into museums and weren't sold to collectors, rumors grew about what Virginia was doing with them.

> I liked to think Virginia
> hoarded them like the dragon
> Mother sometimes referred to her
> as. That much I remember. But it
> turned out that wasn't the case.
> Virginia often lived at Idlewood
> when between adventures.

Of course Virginia lived here! Anna knew that already. But she didn't know anything about a scandal or the Mob!

> My own memories are fuzzy. I
> recall playing hide-and-seek
> with my aunt Virginia in the
> early summer of 1925 when a
> crowd of angry people stomped
> up to the house, cutting the
> game short. But before my mother

passed away, she told me the
whole truth. Police and other
anti-corruption agents had
busted a Mob family near
Washington, D.C. In the raid,
they turned up a number of
interesting items, including a
jade-and-gold statue of the
Buddha that, famously, Virginia
had brought home from China. I've
included a copy of the newspaper
clipping about the Buddha.

The clipping had been copied along with the letter.
Anna touched the picture of Virginia holding a statue
that, even in the black-and-white picture, gleamed like
gold.

How could that statue have wound up in the posses-
sion of the Mob? The authorities wanted to know, too.
They went to Idlewood to question the family, especially
Virginia, who was currently visiting.

My parents were helpful but
shocked. The police wanted to
search the house, but Virginia
was belligerent. She refused
to allow a search without a
warrant. So the police came
back with one.

June 14, 1925, came. That evening, police searched Virginia's things. Among her belongings, they found a ledger keeping track of treasures she'd brought home. And how much they'd sold for to the Mob.

```
My aunt Virginia was running a
money-laundering business. She
would bring back artifacts from
the countries she visited. Then
she would sell those artifacts
to the Mob, and they could pay
her with money they got from
illegal businesses. She was
free to spend that money as she
pleased, free from any known
connection to the Mob, and the
Mob was free to legitimately
sell the treasures and pocket
the clean money from their sales.
That way, they could use that
money without the government
wondering where they got it
if it seemed too much for any
legitimate business to earn.
Their one mistake was selling
the famous Buddha statue. It was
too well known.
```

That discovery unleashed a number of questions for the police. If Virginia Maines was selling her treasures to the Mob, what else was she doing for them? Was she smuggling alcohol into the States (which was illegal at the time)? Was she smuggling weapons on her plane? How many people had been hurt because of her? Were those treasures gifts like she claimed, or were they stolen?

Anna's gut clenched. No! Virginia couldn't have stolen those items. No way!

Simon's letter continued.

> Virginia, of course, insisted she was innocent. But the statue, the ledger, and her belligerence when questioned seemed like too much proof. The police left Idlewood, convinced Virginia was guilty. Mother had been furious with my aunt. I vaguely remember them shouting in the entry hall. "You've shamed yourself and us!" Mother had said. The shouting continued until late in the evening. I held a pillow against my ears, but I could still hear it.
>
> The next morning, Virginia was gone.

Anna knew the story. Not even her clothing had been taken with her. And no one ever found a single one of her treasures again.

The rest of the letter flowed past Anna's eyes. Virginia's flight was proof enough to the police that she was guilty. When she never appeared, her case was closed, the official story being that she must have died in the mountains, whether by wild animal, injury, or sheer exposure, no one knew. After all, Virginia Maines had never been foolish enough, before, to brave the wilderness without supplies. This time, perhaps, the lack of preparation finished her. The Gardners, ashamed, never publicly spoke of Virginia again. The ledger went missing before the police could take it, and Mr. Gardner used his influence to keep the police from speaking out about the case, so all reports of it were lost, probably destroyed. They preferred for people to remember Virginia as a hero but to forget that she was related to the family at Idlewood. Which was exactly what happened. And not long after, the Gardners sold Idlewood, and the scandal was buried even deeper.

```
That's why I was so surprised
when I got your letter. The
secret had been just that for
so long, but I suppose now it's
time for the truth. Mother never
imagined her own sister could
have ever been wrapped up with
the Mob, but she was wrong. The
hero Virginia Maines was nothing
more than a thief and a criminal.
```

A spot of water hit the page.

Anna blinked back another tear. "It's not true," she said. So what if the letter was written by an actual member of the Gardner family? Ginny was innocent. She had to be. It wasn't like anyone had any proof that she did any of these things.

These are the memories of someone who was there. He said his parents told him the story, and they would know. Why would they lie? You know she lived here, and you know she disappeared. Maybe this is why. Because she was selling her treasures to the Mob. She stole her treasures, and she sold them.

"I would *never* do that!" Anna announced to the empty room.

But you aren't Virginia, she told herself. *And Ginny liked to court danger.*

Her hero, Virginia Maines, a thief? A Mob accomplice? It couldn't possibly be true.

And yet, there it was, staring at her in black and white.

◆ ◆ ◆

Numbers. Charlie needed numbers. And yet he kept revisiting the same places he'd found messages before. The upstairs hall. The library. Hoping somehow a new list of code numbers would appear there.

Then again, Charlie thought, remembering how the bookcase shook, maybe they could. Anything could happen in this house. Maybe not ghosts . . . but something.

Why was he doing this? He wasn't even sure he was

supposed to be looking for a book code! For all he knew, he was chasing the wrong trail. But he kept carrying the book, searching through it and through the house, because what other choice did he have?

He had a puzzle, and he needed to know what the puzzle was for. It would bug him forever to leave Idlewood not knowing the solution. What message did it mean to tell him, and why?

And who had left it? Charlie thought it was Mr. Silver, the overseer of the renovations. But no matter how much he read about the house in the library, he could never figure out why Silver would leave a message.

Emily knew Idlewood so well; maybe she would know why a code had been left in the walls. Maybe she'd even be able to see the changes made during the renovation!

So Charlie stopped wandering aimlessly through the halls and began a real search. He started at the ballroom; she'd been there earlier. "Hello?" he called, his voice echoing in the big room. "Anyone here?"

A figure rose from one of the armchairs. But it was only Mr. Llewellyn. "Sorry," Charlie called. "I'm looking for Emily."

Mr. Llewellyn frowned. "Why?" Then, folding his arms, the man added, "I mean, it looks like you're about to do some reading, though I recommend you go outside. It's a lovely day. Most of the other guests are spending their afternoon by the pond."

If they're out there, then why are you in here? But then

again, Mr. Llewellyn was the owner. If he wanted to sit inside, that was his right.

Charlie shook his head. "Done reading. Have you seen Emily?"

"Not since lunch." Mr. Llewellyn took a step toward Charlie and craned his neck. "Is your sister with you?"

Charlie shook his head.

"Where is she?" Mr. Llewellyn asked.

"These days, I have no idea. But as long as no one's yelling, it's okay, right?" Charlie asked. "I'll go check outside. She's probably out there." He shut the door to the ballroom and hurried to put the book in his bedroom.

Charlie had spent the whole morning looking for that copy of *Treasure Island*, so he hadn't had a chance to enjoy the weather. But Mr. Llewellyn was right: The day was warm and not too humid, not after yesterday's rain.

He'd also been right that everyone else was out, enjoying the grounds. The women's tour group wandered in pairs or trios, occasionally stopping to rub more sunblock on. The young family was playing "Duck, Duck, Goose" on the grass. Rosie and Xavier were nowhere to be seen—they must be hiking the Appalachian Trail again.

There were Emily's parents, out walking the small gardens on the east side of the house. Charlie waved at them. Maybe he should ask them about the clue. They were Emily's parents; they might know the house's history as well as she did, or even better.

But Charlie's parents didn't much care for codes, and

Anna certainly didn't. Maybe Emily was the only history geek in the family. Besides, imagining himself telling an adult about the numbers and messages he'd found made Charlie a little queasy. What if they thought what he was doing was wrong? What if they stopped him from looking for the numbers?

Emily, though, was his age. She might be interested, especially about the book and the history. Hey, what if she'd found numbers, in groups of three, around the house somewhere? What luck would that be?

Charlie couldn't find Emily anywhere on the front side of the house, or on the east side. He didn't think she'd be in the west parking lot, but the expansive lands to the back . . . maybe. Charlie hadn't explored that area yet, though he was sure Anna must have. He passed Sunglasses Woman, who crouched and yelled, "Give a little warning before you run around corners like that!"

"Sorry!" Charlie didn't slow.

Around the back was the forest of evergreens he'd seen from the house. Could Emily be in there? Charlie wasn't sure how, since the trees were densely grown. He tried to squeeze between two of them and got a branch in the mouth for his efforts.

As he circled the trees, he couldn't help thinking: This house, with its codes and secrets . . . wouldn't it make sense that the weird forest in the backyard wasn't just an old, overgrown grove but a puzzle itself?

When Charlie found the gap between the trees, he wasn't surprised at all. "A maze," he whispered, and headed inside. Whether or not Emily was in here (and he didn't know why she wouldn't be because mazes were cool!), *he* wanted to explore it.

Ha! He was like Anna. Only, and his heart sank, not really. A maze invited exploration. Anna explored even the places that wanted to keep her out, and wasn't that what made her brave?

But still, a maze was a maze. So Charlie stepped into the cool shade of the trees.

The maze smelled sweet, almost citrusy. He wondered what kind of trees made up the walls. He'd have to remember what they looked like and search for pictures online once he got home.

The maze, though small, was surprisingly intricate. Twists and turns appeared almost constantly, making Charlie backtrack often. Not that he minded. He just added each dead end to the mental map in his head and used the shadow of Idlewood, falling over half the paths, as a guide to what parts of the maze he hadn't visited yet.

He'd have to bring Anna here, though she'd probably already explored it. Where was she? If she wasn't out on the grounds, and she wasn't wreaking havoc in the house, then where?

He wasn't the only guest in the maze. The honeymooners giggled as they ran past him, a few times (they seemed to get lost a lot), and Charlie found an elderly couple wandering the maze. The woman, the one with wild curly gray hair, was smiling into the sunlight, and her mustachioed husband wore a bemused expression.

"Don't get too turned around, kid!" he said when he spotted Charlie. "You don't want to be out here all night."

"I won't be," Charlie said. By his calculations, he was approaching the center of the maze. What would be there? In the old movies his mom liked to watch, there was usually something in the middle of a hedge maze. A fountain, or maybe a gazebo, or—

"Huh?" Charlie turned a corner to find Suitcase Man standing in the center of the maze, pinned suitcase by his side, staring at the ground with a stick in his hand. Other than him, the center of the maze was empty.

Suitcase Man snapped his head up to face Charlie. "Oh, you," he said, sliding the stick behind him. "Um, you're . . ."

"Charlie Henderson."

"Nice to meet you, kid. Jack Argent."

Charlie peered at the stick in the man's hand. "What are you doing?"

Mr. Jack Argent grinned, stepping away from the boy. "Just out enjoying this maze. I have to say, I was surprised to find it. I don't think it was mentioned in any of the literature on the house, do you?"

Charlie shrugged. He took another step closer as the "stick" behind Mr. Argent's back let out a whir. He glanced at the disk on its end. "Is that a metal detector?"

"Why don't you keep going? The maze must have an end. I bet a smart kid like you could find it quickly."

Charlie looked at the man. He was still grinning, but

his eyes were wider than normal. *He looks scared.* "Why do you have a metal detector?"

"Um, well," Mr. Argent stammered, but Charlie's mood started to lift. It seemed like Mr. Argent might know something he didn't! Maybe he'd found the numbers, and maybe he knew what they led to.

"Did you find something?" Charlie asked, taking in the pins on the man's suitcase. England, Quebec, Arizona, Oregon . . . Mr. Argent had traveled a lot. What had he looked for, and found, in those places? "Did the . . . did the clues lead you out here?"

Was that clear enough? Or, if Mr. Argent wasn't following the same clues he was, was it vague enough?

Mr. Argent scratched his head, then shook it and swung the metal detector out from behind him. "I guess you could say they did."

"I knew it!" Charlie leaped into the air. "How did you find them? *Where* did you find them? And do you have a copy of the book, too? I bet you got yours from the library, because I couldn't find one there."

Mr. Argent raised a hand. "Whoa, slow down." He rested the metal detector against his leg. "Book? I don't know what you're talking about."

"Oh." Charlie took a step back. "I, uh, thought . . ." He swallowed. So Mr. Argent wasn't following a book code. "Why are you out here?"

Mr. Argent frowned. "Are you going to tell Mr. Llewellyn?"

Honestly, Charlie wanted to stutter an apology and

leave. But something didn't add up, not with Idlewood and not with Mr. Argent. So he straightened up and pretended, for a moment, that he was Anna. "Why would I? Are you doing something wrong?"

"No, of course not! There's nothing illegal . . . I mean, this is for the greater good."

"Okay. So, what are you looking for?" When Mr. Argent didn't answer, Charlie added, "I bet I could help you find it. I'm pretty good at solving things. My family is here because I won a math competition. And if I can't, there's always Mr. Llewellyn."

"Inquisitive type, aren't you?" But Mr. Argent was smiling. "Let's just say that the gold and jewels of Idlewood aren't all sitting on display in there."

It took Charlie half a second to realize what Mr. Argent meant. "You're looking for treasure? Are you serious?"

Mr. Argent nodded, and Charlie looked around. "But why? Don't tell me pirates used to bury their loot here, in the Shenandoah Mountains."

"Pirates?" Mr. Argent laughed, and Charlie's face got warm. He'd been thinking too much about *Treasure Island.*

"No, nothing like that," Mr. Argent said. "Or, well, maybe. Could have been pirates, could have just been old mobsters or moonshiners. Honestly, I don't really care as long as the treasure is still around."

"You still haven't told me why you think there's treasure here."

Mr. Argent laughed. "Family history, mainly. A story

passed down from someone who used to work on the house. Supposedly, there's riches on the property, and the Gardners knew about it, so when they sold the house, they left clues behind to tell people—probably their friends or family—where it was. I heard Idlewood was opening up for the first time in decades, and I already had made plans to come, so I thought, might as well see if anyone found it yet."

Whoa. "So you're out here with a metal detector looking for the treasure?"

"A big maze without a fountain or something in the middle? I thought this would be a perfect hiding place." Mr. Argent sighed. "Look, Charlie. If I know about the treasure, I'm sure someone else does, too. Maybe Mr. Llewellyn, or maybe just one of the other guests. And since I only have this weekend to search, I'd appreciate it if you didn't tell anyone what I'm doing. Just keep it a secret for one more day, okay?"

Charlie's head was spinning. Treasure? Here? "Okay," he managed to say.

Mr. Argent nodded. "Thank you. Anyway, think you could help me? Let me know if you see anything that might help me find it?"

"Um, sure. Okay." Charlie nodded, still feeling a bit bowled over by Mr. Argent's information. "See you around. I need to go."

Charlie turned and raced out of the maze, feet moving almost as fast as his mind. Treasure. *Here.* He believed it. Why wouldn't he? No one left clues and puzzles for no good reason. And a rich family protecting its wealth?

That made sense, too. All this time, the misplaced numbers and codes on the wall were leading him to treasure. *Treasure Island.* Mr. Silver! Probably wasn't even his real name! This was a treasure hunt. It always had been.

Charlie figured he *could* tell Mr. Argent about the codes and share the message, but then he reconsidered: After all, Mr. Argent had a hunch and a metal detector, but Charlie had the codes. He could find the treasure easily, once he had the numbers for the book code.

Charlie barely saw the Idlewood grounds as he found his way out of the maze and raced back to the house. Instead, he saw visions of gold and silver, and himself the brave champion who found them. Doing something more than just sitting in a chair, reading about elaborate codes that had no purpose. Wouldn't Anna be impressed!

Mr. Argent could keep looking, and so could all the other guests if they wanted. But Charlie was going to be the one to find the treasure. All he had to do was find the numbers for the book code, and he had the entire afternoon to look.

12

WELL, THAT SEARCH *was a waste of time.* After Charlie left the maze, he'd searched for Anna first, excited to tell her about how there was treasure hidden here. But Anna wasn't anywhere, so he tried looking for Emily to ask her if she knew about the treasure and tell her about the book code. They could look for the code numbers together.

But after searching for Emily in the main rooms and going up and knocking on the Rome suite door and getting no answer, Charlie had gone back outside only to find Emily's parents had disappeared, too.

"I think I saw them heading into the forest," Rosie had told him when he'd asked around. "I'm sure they'll be back by dinner."

Forced to wait, Charlie wandered back to the China suite, passing the older woman with the curly hair. She smiled at him and offered him a candy from her big bag, but Charlie declined.

Inside the family's suite, Anna's door was closed. She must have come back to her room, the one place he hadn't thought to look. Why would she be home when there was so much to do? The place was quiet. Maybe she was napping. That was unlike her.

The Henderson parents must have been out somewhere, maybe talking to Mr. Llewellyn about the house's history. Lots of the adults seemed to be eager to do that.

There was still a little time until dinner would be served. He could take *Treasure Island* out into the halls and search for the numbers one more time.

Charlie went to his room and touched the sword for good luck. Grinning, he swiped his finger down the dull edge, imagining what it might have been like sharp. Had this sword been part of the treasure haul? Or maybe something used to defend it, once upon a time?

Wow. Treasure! He wanted to sit on the bed and daydream, picturing the heaps of gems somewhere on the property. But doing that wouldn't get him any closer to finding said heaps of gems. So he needed his book.

Which, he was sure, he'd left on the little table beside his bed. But now all that was there was his glasses case.

Charlie knelt, checking around the table. Had the book fallen off? It wasn't on the floor, and it hadn't slid under his bed.

Maybe he'd left it downstairs. But no, he remembered

carrying it back to the room after Mr. Llewellyn had commented on it. So, could it be in the suite's living room? Maybe he'd left it on a table there?

After about ten minutes spent ransacking the living room, yanking cushions off the couch, and sorting through every item on every shelf, Charlie had to set the second dragon statue back in its place and admit defeat: *Treasure Island* was gone.

He dropped onto the couch and put his head in his hands. The only copy in Idlewood, and he knew because he'd looked so hard for it. He *knew* he'd put it here. So someone must have moved it. But who?

Another treasure hunter? *If I know about the treasure, I'm sure someone else does, too,* Mr. Argent had said. Who else might be looking for it?

Mr. Llewellyn? He was the owner of Idlewood. If anyone knew about the hidden treasure, it was him, and he had seen Charlie with the book.

Then again, so had Rosie and Xavier. They seemed so nice, but it could be a cover.

Charlie's stomach felt cold. He'd carried *Treasure Island* around the whole house, examining it all morning. Anyone could have seen him with it. Mr. Argent. Matching T-Shirts family. The old man with the mustache, or the woman with the curly hair. The honeymooners. The tour group. If they knew about the treasure, and had any idea that a book code was needed, they'd know he had the book. He hadn't exactly been subtle.

But that was only because he'd had no idea, until now, what he was looking for!

A door opened and closed. Anna emerged from her room, red-eyed and silent. She looked at him.

"Charlie?" she asked. "I thought I heard you come and go earlier." She shrugged, and headed toward the bathroom.

Wait a minute. Wait one darn minute. Anna was nosy. Anna was a troublemaker. Who knew how much time she'd spent exploring the house? How much she might know? What if she'd figured out there was treasure here and how to scoop its discovery out from under him?

Anna, his sister who lived in the same suite and knew he had a copy of *Treasure Island*. Who had been vanishing for hours at a time with no explanation for where she'd been. And who could easily get the book, even when the suite's door was locked.

Anna left the bathroom, rubbing one eye, and stopped to look at him. "Hey," she said. "Where have you been all day?"

"I could ask you the same thing," Charlie said.

Anna frowned. The redness of her eyes pricked at Charlie's senses, but he ignored it. He needed to get answers *now*, not piece together clues like he always did. Look where that had gotten him.

"Um, I've been in my room," Anna said.

"But before that?" Charlie walked forward so he was face-to-face with his big sister. He'd be anxious if he wasn't so furious. "This morning? And what about yesterday? Where do you go, and why are you always taking showers?"

Anna crossed the hall and stood in front of her door. "I've been exploring the grounds."

"Oh, yeah?"

"Yeah. You look upset. Did you have a fight with Emily or something?"

Charlie scowled. "Where is it?"

Anna shuffled her feet. "Where is what?"

But those red-rimmed eyes darted back into her room. Charlie pushed past her and saw a book on the bed, but more importantly, the brown paper wrapping. "Is that Emily's book?"

"She came by earlier to see our rooms. She left it behind. I was just reading it."

Charlie picked up the book. Emily carried this everywhere. It wasn't something she'd just leave behind. And Anna reading a math book for fun? Please.

"I don't believe you," he whispered.

"What?" Anna stepped into her room.

Charlie turned around. "I don't believe you," he said, louder. "I think you took this book from her."

"That's ridiculous! Why would I do that?" Now it wasn't just Anna's eyes that were red; spots of color appeared on her cheeks. Even the curls in her ponytail looked tense, ready to spring loose.

"I don't know. Why did you take my copy of *Treasure Island*?" Charlie asked.

Anna's mouth opened and closed. She squeezed her

eyes shut and said, "If you're referring to that dusty old book you've been toting around all day, I didn't touch it."

"Liar!" Charlie threw Emily's textbook down on the bed. "It's gone."

"Did you grab it when you were here earlier? Maybe you left it downstairs."

"I didn't come back here after lunch at all," Charlie said. "So that's not going to work."

Anna frowned. "Really? Because . . ." She shook her head. "Maybe you lost it. Or are you so brilliant that you never lose anything?" She glared at him.

"I didn't lose it. I know I put it right by my bed, and now it's gone. Who else can get into this room, Anna? Just our family. I know it was you."

"It wasn't me! Why don't you trust me?"

"You know why!"

Anna stepped backward, like Charlie's words had physically hit her. Then she rallied, taking in a large breath, which she released with a yell. "Gah! Fine, you know what? Fine. Why not? Every time there's a problem, why not blame Anna? You could have figured that Mom or Dad found it and returned it to the library, but no. *I* have to have been the thief. Just because I'm the screwup, right?"

Charlie hadn't considered that his parents might have moved it. But that wasn't the point. "Maybe if you weren't always causing trouble, we wouldn't think that. Why do you have to be so reckless?"

"I'm not reckless. I just . . . there's so much more. You

don't understand. How could you understand? You're too scared of the world to step out from behind your books."

Charlie felt like he'd been slapped. "That's not true."

"Isn't it? Why don't you ask Mom and Dad where your book is? They'd be the ones to know."

"Mom and Dad have been out all afternoon. You've been here. Or at least, I think you have. Maybe you've been off wherever it is you go. Where do you go, Anna?"

"Nowhere special."

"Really? Then why did you take my book? What have you seen? What do you *know*?"

Anna didn't say anything. She just opened the door behind her and ran. Charlie chased her as she fled the suite, closing the door on him, which slowed him down.

"Come back here!" he called. If he had any doubt Anna was the thief, it had fled as soon as Anna did. Innocent people didn't run. Everyone knew that.

His sister's red hair flashed as she left the entry hall of Idlewood and dashed out into the sun. Charlie caught a glimpse of her turning right before she vanished outside.

Gasping for air (Anna was the athlete), Charlie stumbled after her. When he couldn't see her on the lawn, he turned the corner of the house to check the side. No sign of his sister.

He'd guessed wrong. She must have run out into the trees. Well, good riddance. *You're too scared of the world to step out from behind your books.* Oh, yeah? Once he found that treasure, she'd see he wasn't too scared to do anything important. He'd show her.

Or, he could have, if Anna hadn't taken that book. Now he was exactly as useless as she thought he was. And she was just as selfish and destructive as everyone said *she* was.

Charlie went back inside, short one key to a code and one thieving sister.

13

ANNA, UP ON THE ROOF, watched her brother scan the Idlewood grounds for her and then turn to leave. If he had just looked up, he would have seen her. But people didn't usually look up. They didn't bother to look for things that weren't right in front of their faces.

Like that she *didn't* steal Charlie's old book. Why would she want it? And even if she had borrowed it, why would she lie about it? Trust Charlie to value some stupid book over his own sister.

Bitter, Anna climbed the rest of the tower to the window, imagining all the things she should have said to Charlie instead of running away. But would any of it have mattered? Anna was the reckless child, and to her parents—and apparently Charlie, too—that meant delinquent.

She wasn't! Just because she liked to explore and find new places, try new things, didn't mean she didn't have any kind of moral compass.

So breaking into a secret area is okay?

That was different. There was no reason the third floor should be off-limits. But stealing was always wrong. She knew that. Why didn't anyone else think she did?

Why wasn't there anyone, anywhere, in the world who understood her?

Hopping into the dusty tower bedroom, Anna looked around at all the maps and charts left behind by Ginny Maines, explorer and fallen hero.

It *wasn't* true, what that letter said. Simon had been a child, and everything had been told to him later. Maybe he and his mother got it wrong. Virginia Maines wasn't a criminal. Anna knew her. She'd read her journal and letters. And, more than that, she and Ginny had an understanding. They were the same. Anna knew the difference between right and wrong. That meant Ginny must have, too.

All Anna had to do was find proof. She sat at the desk and picked up the journal, flipping through the water-stained pages to the last entries. The ones right before Ginny vanished. If she'd left her own story behind, it would be here.

1924, 1925 . . . June.

"That was a wonderful trip to India," Ginny had written in early June 1925. "I know I said that about my recent trip back to China, but it is true. I am so lucky to have such great friends who are so kind to me. They came to watch me board the <u>Dragon</u> and fly home. I leave India a piece of my heart, but I admit, I've taken

182

more than my share of treasure back with me. Soon I'll
be back home with Elaine and her sweet children."

And that was it. The paragraph ended, and the next was blank. All the rest of the journal was blank.

An innocent person would want to tell their story, wouldn't they? Feeling sick, Anna set the journal back on the desk.

Standing, she looked around the room. The letter had said that Virginia vanished the day after the police found incriminating evidence against her. They thought she had run away. Had she? Why didn't she bring any of her things with her? There had to be more to the story.

The evidence! The letter had said the ledger disappeared, but Virginia famously hadn't taken anything with her. So those records might be here. If Anna could find them, then she would know for sure.

Dropping to her knees, she searched the dusty floor. As scattered as it was with old papers and books, she had to be careful not to destroy what she touched, and to find the right evidence.

Maps of India. Lists of plane parts needed for repairs. A note from Bradley detailing Maori cultural customs. Friendly letters from all over the globe. Anna found these and more while ransacking Virginia's tower room, looking for the missing ledger.

It shouldn't be this hard. After all, she'd already searched the room looking for those letters from Elaine.

Anna froze. Hadn't she seen stacks of papers covered in numbers?

Heart racing, she made her way down the stairs, down to the stacks of papers beside a toppled chair where she had found one of Elaine's letter. There they were. The pages were loose, haphazardly stacked, but they were faceup. Time had faded the ink on the page, but even so, Anna knew the handwriting. She had seen it scrawled across page after journal page.

She picked up the top sheet and carefully blew away the dust to reveal the ledger page beneath. Columns of numbers, and to the left of them, notes about what each sum was for.

Anna ignored the money. She didn't care how much each item was worth. It was the list of items that concerned her. It covered the page.

Wooden African mask.

Gold Celtic armband.

And, toward the bottom, but not the last entry . . . jade Buddha.

Anna let the page fall from her hands. It was Virginia's handwriting. She was certain.

Virginia Maines was a criminal. It was all true. Anna sank to the grimy floor. Her throat tightened and stung.

They had been so alike. At least, Anna had thought so. When she read Virginia's journal, it was like reading her own mind, scribbled down before her eyes. Virginia had understood what it felt like to want to fly above the clouds, to explore every corner (especially the off-limits ones), to itch and ache and yearn for something more. Anna had loved her for it.

But maybe that ache was what drove her to crime. After a while, maybe exploring jungles and tombs wasn't exciting enough anymore. Maybe the Mob became interesting to Virginia.

Anna had that same itch. She could feel it, even now under the deadweight of the realization that her hero was a crook. That desire to poke around and know more.

The same itch that got her in trouble in school made it so her parents and brother didn't trust her. And she'd thought Ginny had been just like her. But Anna was not a criminal. So what did *that* mean?

The successful explorer who had shared Anna's every quirk was a lie. Maybe there was no one like Anna. The world was full of Mr. Llewellyns and Charlies, good, quiet people who expected so little from life. After all, the world was mapped, plotted, photographed from space. What was left for people with that itch for discovery when everything could already be seen and read about in books or online? Why travel when every question could be answered from the comfort of your room?

Anna understood now. She was abnormal, and she needed to push that . . . fine, that *reckless* behavior down inside herself. Quell it, lock it away, before it got her into more trouble. If no one was like her, if no one understood, then the problem had to be *her*, right?

Her legs feeling as heavy as her heart, Anna trudged back to the top of the tower. In a haze, she pulled herself out the window and climbed down the tower, and then down the side of the house. She jumped from the ledge to land in the grass with a thump.

"Did you just climb down from there?"

Anna turned around. Mr. Llewellyn was standing right behind her. "Young lady," he said. "Did you hear me? I asked you if you were climbing on that wall."

Anna shrugged. Yesterday, she might have come up with some good excuse or retort to fling back. But today, she just felt tired.

"Don't lie to me. Mr. Haskell said he saw you up on the roof," Mr. Llewellyn said. "Poking around guest rooms is one thing, but going up there . . . Come with me." He grabbed Anna's shoulder and steered her back into Idlewood.

Anna didn't resist. She'd been caught, just like Virginia. The only difference was she couldn't disappear, so it was time to take her punishment.

The Hendersons were in the dining room, waiting for dinner to be served, Charlie included. Mr. Llewellyn dragged Anna in front of them.

"Anna? Where have you been?" her mother said, pulling Anna out of Mr. Llewellyn's grip. "We've been looking for you. You need to give Charlie his book back."

Anna didn't say anything. What was the use in protesting that she hadn't taken the book? Everyone had already decided she had.

"I found her climbing down from the roof," Mr. Llewellyn said. "I don't think I need to tell you how dangerous that is."

Anna's family gaped at her. "The roof?" Charlie asked.

"What were you doing up there?" Her father folded his arms.

"I think we all know what she was doing up there," her mother said. "Thank you for bringing her back safely," she said to Mr. Llewellyn.

"My pleasure," he said, sounding like he meant the opposite. "I'm sorry to inconvenience you, but I must ask you to carefully chaperone your daughter for the last day of your vacation. We don't want her getting into further trouble."

"Of course," Anna's father said. "Don't worry. One of us will be watching her at all times."

Anna bristled. "You don't have to do that!"

"Yeah, they do," Charlie said.

"Charlie," their mother warned, but to Anna, she said, "You haven't exactly given us a choice."

Mr. Llewellyn coughed. "Well, if this is settled, I have other places I need to be."

"Yes, thank you," Anna's mother said, and Mr. Llewellyn left.

Anna's mother launched into a lecture about safety and privacy and "we don't know what we're going to do with you" and "you need to give Charlie back his book." Anna let it wash over her like a wave, nodding at appropriate times.

When her mom stopped, Anna asked, "Can I just go back to the suite?"

"It will be dinner soon."

"I'm not hungry."

Her mom stopped. Her frown smoothed. "Are you feeling all right?" she asked gently.

"I just don't want dinner."

"All right."

Anna left the dining room and went upstairs. She could hear her father behind her, missing dinner but making good on his promise that Anna would not be left alone for the rest of the weekend. But she didn't care. She could smell beef cooking from down the hall, but it didn't wake her appetite.

Anna went to her room and sprawled on her bed. Her head filled with ledger listings, old female explorers, and the invisible gulf that separated her from all the people around her, she couldn't feel much of anything at all.

❖ ❖ ❖

It was very late by the time Emily made it back to her room. After translating the Roman numerals to normal, Arabic numbers and writing them on the back of one of the Polaroids (it was the only thing resembling scratch paper that she had with her), she'd realized that she was missing her book about Idlewood.

Emily couldn't remember where she'd left it. She swore she'd had it downstairs, when she was looking at the paintings and how they'd all been altered. But after that, she couldn't remember holding it anymore. So she went back down to the ballroom to search.

It wasn't there. She'd checked on every small table and shelf (a few of which seemed a little emptier than she remembered) and around and under every nailed-down chair. She'd retraced her footsteps six times. Her book was gone.

Where could it be? For a heart-stopping moment, she wondered if Mr. Llewellyn had found it, or Suitcase Man, the wall-tapper. That book had a letter hidden inside that Emily wasn't supposed to have! And those pages could give people the wrong idea, especially if they'd heard of Virginia's treasure. If they found out *she* may have lived here for a time . . .

Maybe someone had seen the book and put it "back" in the library. Yeah, that had to be it. Emily dashed to the library and spent a good amount of time tearing it apart (figuratively speaking, of course; Emily would never rip up a book) before her parents found her and made her come with them to dinner.

Though the food was excellent, as always, Emily fidgeted in her seat, aching to go back to look for the book.

She tried to keep herself calm by looking for the short lady she'd seen examining the carved door's lock. Not an easy task: Many of the tour group members were short. Even Rosie wasn't all that tall. Mr. Mustache's wife seemed to have the same look as the woman she'd seen—her hair was also gray and curly—but she looked a bit too tall. The more Emily looked, the less sure she was that *any* of them were the woman she'd seen.

After dinner, although Emily tried to make an

escape, she was pushed to join in a night of pastimes that had been popular in the 1920s. In the parlor, an old-fashioned radio played an episode of some adventure show, and most of the adult guests listened to it or read books. Book Lady, of course, was reading. Mr. Llewellyn sat by a stack of board games. The T-Shirts family had taken one of them and was playing tiddlywinks, though one of the children was edging toward the Sunglasses Couple. Mr. Mustache's wife came in late, having left her huge purse in her room and feeling the need to retrieve it. She came back with her bag and a huge smile, and Emily was jealous. It was so easy for adults to do what they wanted to!

Charlie was there, eyeing a Ouija board and running a finger along the earpiece of his glasses. Despite her annoyance with being stuck here with everyone, Emily had to laugh. A house this old? Everyone always thought there were ghosts.

Maybe a ghost stole her book. Ha!

Charlie eventually joined the young family in their game, and Emily considered joining them, too, just to have something to do. But it really didn't interest her to flip around little plastic disks, so she just flopped onto a sofa to wait out the night.

A T-shirted child was opening Sunglasses Woman's purse. Emily wondered how long it would take for the kid's parents to stop her.

Anna was sitting on the sofa, too, gripping the arm like it was a life raft. When she saw Emily, she gave something that could be a nod or a shrug and then rested her head against the cushions.

Wow. Even while getting dragged down the hall by an angry Mr. Llewellyn, Anna had been fighting back. This seemed very . . . out of character. "Tired?" Emily asked.

Anna's mouth twitched. "You could say that. My parents made me come."

"Same. I'd rather be in my room, reading."

Or trying to figure out what had sets of three numbers each until her brain melted into a pool of peanut butter.

Anna sat up and faced Emily. "Oh," she said. "You left your book in my room. Your . . . math book."

Emily sagged with relief. "*That's* where it is," she said. "I've been looking all day."

"You can come by and get it later," Anna said. "It's just on my bedside table." She returned to leaning on the sofa's arm.

"Thanks, I will." Emily scratched her head. "Hey."

"What?" Anna sat up again.

"Did you read my book, by any chance? It's just that you paused when you called it a math book."

"Yeah. About that. Why would you disguise a history book like that?" Anna tugged at a loose curl. "I mean, it's about Idlewood. This is Idlewood. If there's ever a good place to read something like that, it's here."

"Well, I'm supposed to be doing math homework," Emily said. "Hence the disguise. But I wanted to read up on the house while we're here."

Anna grinned. "You disguised an educational book as another educational book?"

Emily scowled. "I like history. I take after my parents in that way. They're historians, and they do great work. I'm proud of them."

That was a little more truth than Emily meant to reveal, but before she could detect Anna's reaction, there was a yell as the Sunglasses Woman snatched up her purse. The T-Shirt kid's parents grabbed her, while the child cried, "Want cookie!"

The Sunglasses Woman stood and left the room, purse in hand, the T-Shirt parents whispered to their child, and the room reordered itself.

"I bet they're proud of you," Anna said, sinking back down into the sofa. "Your parents. Following in their footsteps like that."

"I hope so."

Anna traced the embroidery. "Don't we all," she said.

Emily picked at the sofa cushion and then stopped when she realized she was probably defacing an antique. Her parents wouldn't be proud of *that*, for sure. But when she'd deciphered the message Elaine had left for her, they would be. She'd show them that not only could she be the historian they were, but she could prove what even they couldn't. All by herself.

Anna stood. "I'm going to see if there's any dinner left over."

Emily nodded. A moment later, she stood up too and joined the older guests at the radio. Now it was playing jazz, recorded by some of the greats. She recognized Cole Porter; her mother loved him. A little while later, her parents came to collect her.

"That was fun," her mother said as they climbed the stairs. "If it weren't for all the jeans and T-shirts in the crowd, I would have believed we were really back in 1925. I wish we could do this again."

"If we can save Idlewood," her father said in a hushed voice as they crossed the threshold to their rooms.

"Right," Emily said. "How's it coming?"

Her mom sighed and glanced at her dad. "Slowly. Mr. Llewellyn must have made some changes when he prepared this house for visitors. Small ones, but there are some things, like moldings and wallpaper, that don't seem quite authentic. It could hurt our position."

Don't worry, Emily thought, smothering a grin. It wouldn't matter how authentic Idlewood was once Elaine's message was solved.

"We're running out of time," Emily's dad said. "Two days down, one to go. I'm documenting all I can, but the later it gets, the weaker our argument seems. I don't know if we can pull this off." He grew silent, obviously thinking about the Muir house.

"I'm sure you can," Emily said. "Anyway, it's late. Good night!"

She hurried back to her room. She had a code to break.

But as soon as she stepped into her lovely white marble room, she knew something was wrong. The room was a mess. Sure, she'd left it that way, but she was pretty sure that when she'd last seen the mound of Polaroids, they'd been on her bed, not on the floor.

Emily felt like a giant hand was squeezing her lungs. She threw herself to the floor and picked up one picture after another, looking for the numbers.

Soon she had a large carpet of white photograph backs in front of her. Every photo accounted for except one. The code was gone.

Wait! She'd written it on her arm. But no! She'd washed it off as soon as she'd transcribed it, thinking it would be safer not to walk around with a bunch of numbers on her skin. If only she'd memorized the code!

As soon as she found out her book was in safe hands, her code went missing. Emily sank to the ground, shoving useless Polaroids out of her way. Someone had come into her room, touched her things, and taken something that belonged to her.

Breathe, Emily. It could be worse. She could just go back to the China suite and get the code again. Anna had said Emily could come by to get her book, so it wouldn't even be weird for her to return.

Emily checked the clock. Past eleven. The Hendersons were probably in bed right now, and her own parents would find it strange if she rushed out so late at night. It would have to wait until morning.

Which left the question of who had taken the code in the first place. Suitcase Man, tapping on the walls? The short woman (who Emily had started to think must be

one of the tour group)? Book Lady? Either of the Sunglasses Couple? Mr. Llewellyn? Her own parents?

Couldn't be. The owner and the other guests had
barely seen or talked to Emily all day, and while her parents had been just as parental as always, they had their
own agenda. Emily had been alone.

In fact, other than Anna on the couch, the only person Emily had spoken to all day was Charlie.

She tapped the floor in a steady rhythm. You know,
Charlie had seen her dash out of the ballroom pretty
quick. And it had been a nice day. *Everyone* had been
outside. What was Charlie doing inside the ballroom in
the first place?

Come to think of it, Charlie *had* been acting strange.
While Anna couldn't seem to be found anywhere, Charlie
was *everywhere*. Emily had spotted him in the library, wandering up and down the upstairs hall, prodding things in
the parlor. Kind of like how she herself was everywhere.

Charlie had taken her code! But why? Was he on the
same mission she was, to save Idlewood? Emily doubted
it. Her parents would know if any other Gardner scholars
were here. He could be a treasure hunter, or maybe his
parents were. Items had been disappearing around Idlewood. Someone had come here to get rich. It could be
the Hendersons.

And Charlie was a math whiz! Emily had even talked
to him about it. He'd know what those numbers meant,
if anyone did.

Gritting her teeth, Emily slammed her palms into her

bed. And she'd thought he was a shy, friendly kid! She should have known better: That was her own cover!

First thing tomorrow, she was going to march over to the China suite, get her code back, and explain to Charlie how thoroughly he'd underestimated Emily Shaughnessy.

14

IT HAD BEEN a long, awkward evening for Charlie. Anna sulked all night, and any attempt by either him or his parents to convince her to give up his book hadn't worked at all. They'd even made her let them search her room, and it wasn't there. She just insisted that she hadn't taken it and had gone to bed early.

Charlie couldn't believe it. Everyone knew she'd stolen the book—why was she keeping up the pretense? The book wasn't even his. It belonged to Idlewood. This was worse for her than poking around rooms when people were checking in, or ducking behind a rope at a museum. If she was smart, she'd just apologize and give the book back.

Unless she couldn't because she'd taken it outside and accidentally dropped it in the pond.

The loss of the book felt like a poison ivy rash. All night, Charlie tossed in bed, thinking about the message

that could have been hidden in that book and the treasure it could have led him to. And now it was gone, all
because of his stupid, careless sister.

Finally it was a new day. The last day of the trip
(Charlie scratched the back of his neck), but still. A new
day. Maybe his parents would finally get Anna to give
up *Treasure Island*. Or really punish her for losing it. He
should also tell them Anna had Emily's book.

Charlie's parents had long since gone to breakfast.
Anna hadn't left her room and hadn't responded when her
parents called for them so they could all go down together.
So Charlie had been told to stay there, since Anna wasn't
supposed to be left alone. His parents were supposed to
bring them both breakfast. But they were taking a long
time! Surely Anna would be fine for five minutes while he
grabbed a slice of toast and an apple.

Charlie had barely stepped outside his family's rooms
when a hand grabbed his elbow and yanked, pulling him
away down the hall. "We need to talk," Emily said.

"Oh, okay," Charlie said. What was this about?

Emily came to a stop once they were around the corner, out of sight of anyone heading down to breakfast. "I
know you took it, and I want it back."

"What?" Charlie thought hard. Oh. That had to be
it. "Your book. I'm not the one who took it. Anna has it."

Emily rolled her eyes. "I know. She told me last night.
Turns out I left it in her room when I was touring your
suite."

"Really?" So, Anna *hadn't* stolen Emily's book. Charlie

rubbed his arm where Emily had gripped it. "So, what are you looking for?"

"You know," Emily hissed. She glanced around the empty hall, then leaned forward. "*It.*" When Charlie didn't react, she said, louder, "The list of numbers in my room! You took it and I want it back."

"Numbers? You have numbers?" Charlie's excitement faded quickly when he realized what Emily was actually saying. "I didn't take anything."

"Right. I mean, it's not like you've been running around the house like you're playing hide-and-seek this whole weekend, or like *you're* the only one who saw me in the ballroom yesterday."

Emily was accusing him—*him*, Charlie—of theft? Didn't she know him? He'd never steal! He wasn't like—

"Anna," he said. "She probably took it. She took something from me, too." He tried to move around Emily and head downstairs, but she blocked him.

"It's not Anna."

"You sure?"

"Positive. I've been over it all night. Why would Anna take them? Really, think about it. You're the one who likes numbers and codes. If anyone could figure out that I had the numbers *and* know why they were important, it was you. So give them back."

Charlie stopped. He had to admit, the evidence sounded pretty impressive stacked up like that. He almost believed that he *had* taken the numbers, and he knew he didn't do it.

199

The evidence had seemed so well stacked against Anna, too. But Anna denied taking *Treasure Island*, and it wasn't with her things. And Anna was reckless and had a tendency to rationalize her choices, but as Charlie thought back, she was always ready to admit to what she did. She'd never been a liar. Or a thief.

Charlie's stomach squirmed. Maybe he'd accused Anna as falsely as he was being accused now. Especially if Emily also had something stolen from her.

"Look," he said. "I didn't take your numbers. I swear."

"Then who did?"

He shook his head. "I don't know. But whoever it was, they took something from me, too. I thought it was Anna, but now . . ." He shrugged, innards twisting once again. It felt almost like he'd been punched in the stomach, being falsely accused. And to think he'd done a little punching himself . . . "Now I'm not so sure."

Emily quieted. She leaned against the wall. "What did they take from you?"

"A book."

"A book?" Emily's eyes widened, and an eager smile bent her lips.

"Yeah. *Treasure Island*. A really old copy, the only one in Idlewood. I think it's part of a book code." Charlie fiddled with his glasses. "Sounds crazy, right?"

"No, not at all!" Emily glanced around the corner. Charlie did, too, but it seemed the hall was empty. That was a little strange. Sure, Emily and Charlie were late, but the T-Shirts family and many of the tour group were fast eaters and should be done with breakfast by now, and therefore roaming the house again. "I believe you. The paintings downstairs aren't the same as they were back when Idlewood was the Gardner family's home. They changed, and every picture had a book added to it. Maybe that's connected to the book you found."

"Really?" So he had been right—the book was important! "I'd never guess the paintings had been changed."

"No one would. But then, how did you find the book in the first place? I mean, how did you know it was special?"

So Charlie explained spotting the faded numbers on the doors and solving the code for the message that took him to her family's suite, and how he'd gone there to search for another code. Emily grinned when he told her about the numbers painted into the Rome city scene.

"I'll have to look for them when I go back," she said. "I can't believe I didn't notice that."

"Well, they're pretty small, and I knew what I was looking for," Charlie said. "Anyway, that code told me 'they are safe' and gave me the book title. And that's as far as I got, because I needed numbers in sets of three to solve the book code, and I couldn't find them."

"And I have them," Emily said. "Or I *had* them. But it's okay," she added. "My list was just a copy. I could get the numbers again. They're in your room."

Charlie perked up. "My room?"

"Anna's, actually. But still. With your help, we can get them back."

"But we still don't have the book." Charlie kicked the baseboard. Gently, so as not to dent it, but with frustration. "Without the book, we can't solve the code."

"That exact book?"

"Maybe. Some book codes are edition-sensitive, and if that's the case, then yeah. But even if it's not, there's still no other copy of *Treasure Island* in the house!"

"Do you think that's why they did it?" Emily asked.

"Who?"

"The person who stole your book and my numbers. Do you think they did it to stop us from figuring it out ourselves?"

Charlie thought about it. Mr. Argent had said that there might be other treasure hunters at Idlewood. The Sunglasses Couple was always dashing away from company outside, or for no apparent reason, and Charlie had spotted them huddling around something, hiding it, at least once. And there was that woman with the wild gray hair . . . she *had* been in the hall right before Charlie discovered his book was missing. What if one of them knew he had the book and that Emily had the numbers? They might have taken Emily and Charlie's clues to keep the kids from solving the mystery. Not to mention, they'd have the clues and be able to solve it themselves.

They might have already solved it! "We might be too late," Charlie said.

Emily paled. "We can't be too late. I *have* to be the one to solve this or—"

"Or?"

Emily played with her hair, avoiding Charlie's eyes. Then she said, "Or Idlewood is gone."

"Wait, what?" Charlie waited for Emily to laugh, but she didn't. "What do you mean Idlewood is gone?"

Emily glanced around, then leaned close to Charlie. "Don't tell anyone, but Mr. Llewellyn is selling Idlewood. Right after this weekend."

"WHAT? Why?"

Emily shook her head. "Money, I think. But he's keeping it secret. I don't know why. I *do* know that if he sells it, the house will be harmed, torn down, or refurbished in a way that Elaine Gardner didn't want. That's why my family and I are here. We're trying to keep Idlewood from being lost."

"Okay." A door opened down the hall, and Charlie and Emily both peeked around the corner. The airplane room couple was leaving their suite, talking in low tones. Charlie thought he caught the name "Llewellyn."

The woman fumbled the key to their suite, and it fell to the ground. She crouched to pick it up, and Emily sucked in her breath. Charlie turned to her as the couple went away. "What's wrong?"

"Oh. Nothing." Emily focused back on him. "Just, it's amazing how short some people can look when they bend down."

"Yeah, interesting. Anyway, what can we do? How

are you going to save Idlewood?" If there was a treasure here, and the clues were hidden in the house, then the house couldn't change! It couldn't get torn down!

"Okay," Emily said. "This is going to sound far-fetched, but I think that the clues in the walls—"

Here it comes. She's hunting the treasure, too.

"—are pointing toward a secret message from Elaine Gardner to her sister."

Huh? Charlie frowned. "So, you're not chasing the treasure, then?"

"Treasure? Oh, *that* treasure." Emily shrugged. "I'm not sure there is one. I mean, if the Gardners needed money, they could have easily sold Virginia's souvenirs."

"Wait, wait. Virginia?"

Emily stared at him. "When you said 'treasure,' I thought you were referring to . . . Virginia Maines lived here. This may be where she left her treasures behind."

Charlie gaped. Virginia Maines? Anna's favorite explorer? "She lived here?"

"It's not well known, but then again, neither is the idea that there's treasure. My parents dug up a piece of evidence that suggested she once lived here, and that she may have vanished due to scandal."

Charlie thought of Anna. What would she do if she knew her idol had lived here and might have been caught up in a scandal?

"Anyway," Emily continued, "my parents didn't think the evidence was strong enough to count as historical fact, but I do. I think Elaine meant for the house to stay as it was for Virginia. I just need to prove it. That's all the treasure I need."

There was a loose thread, and Charlie pulled at it. "Are you sure this *isn't* a treasure hunt? If Virginia vanished from here, and her treasures were here, and she didn't take them with her, then they could still be here." He grinned. "'They are safe.' That's what my message said. Don't you think Elaine could be talking about the treasures?"

Emily chewed on her lip, then looked at the wall behind Charlie. She smiled a little. "Maybe," she said. "Just maybe. I don't know what the clues were leading us to, but if it *is* Virginia's treasure, then that would definitely be enough reason the house had to stay the same. But even if it's just Elaine trying to leave a message about Virginia, or if Virginia were involved in the message, that would be enough, too."

"Either way, we still need to solve the puzzle." Charlie glanced down the hall. Still empty. "Let's go back to my room and get your numbers."

"Okay, but we still don't have the book," Emily said.

"Then we'll just have to find it again," Charlie said. Now that Emily had joined his team, bringing her numbers with her, he felt more optimistic. "I'm not going to let some thief stop us from finding that treasure."

◆ ◆ ◆

Anna had been called to breakfast a while ago, but she hadn't answered, although she'd finished getting ready a long time before. She didn't feel hungry, and she'd rather lie on her bed, staring at the ceiling, instead of trying to choke down cereal while her family silently accused her of things she hadn't done. The suite had gone silent, and Anna wondered if, somehow, she was alone.

She had had a hard time sleeping, and when she did, her rest was broken by anxious dreams. The worst was the one where she was Virginia Maines, and Elaine (who had Charlie's glasses) was yelling at her about stealing a priceless gold book and selling it to the Mob. In the dream, Anna ran and ran as people chased her, screaming accusations. She took off in the *Dragon* to escape them, but the plane flew faster and faster until Anna lost control.

She woke up before she could see what happened next.

Some vacation this was turning out to be. The moment she found a place no one had seen in decades, she also found something devastating. If she'd just sat around like her parents and brother, she'd be bored but not heartbroken. Maybe that was why they did it. It was better to be bored.

Anna sighed and then sat straight up as Charlie and Emily burst through the door.

"See?" Charlie said. "Told you she'd be awake."

"What do you want?" Anna asked. She jumped off the bed and approached her brother. "I thought you went to breakfast."

"Mom and Dad are bringing it up to us," Charlie said.

Of course. Anna had been left in the care of her little brother, again. She nodded to Emily. "I know what you're here for. Your book is right over there."

"That's not—but okay," Emily said. She passed by Anna to where her parents' book sat on the side table, then opened it to the letter tucked inside, smiled, and closed it.

Anna turned her attention back to Charlie. "I don't have it," she said. "Just like all the million other times you asked."

"I know," Charlie said. He was staring at his shoes. "I'm sorry."

"Huh?"

"I was wrong. You didn't take the book. I shouldn't have accused you without proof. And . . . I should have known better. You're not a thief or a criminal or anything like that. So, I'm sorry." He looked up at his sister and stuck out a hand. "Are we okay?"

Anna, mouth hanging slightly open, stared at Charlie's hand. Part of her wanted to scream that *No, we're not okay!* Charlie had made her whole evening miserable because he'd blamed her for something she didn't do and wouldn't accept anything she said.

But the other part had heard Charlie—perfect, math genius Charlie—admit that he was wrong. For once, the image of the golden boy had cracked, and inside Anna could see the brother she'd once had so much fun with. No one was perfect. Not Virginia, not Charlie, and certainly not herself. Maybe it was time someone in this house got a second chance. Might as well be Charlie.

So she reached out and shook his hand. "Don't ever do that again. But yeah, we're okay."

Charlie brightened. "Great. Because we need to use your room."

"What? Why?" But Charlie had already passed Anna and was standing beside Emily, who, book tucked under one arm, was examining the paintings hanging around Anna's bed. "That's a one," she was saying. "I remember it from earlier."

"Anyone going to tell me what's going on?" Anna asked. "It *is* my room."

Charlie and Emily turned to Anna. "I don't know if you noticed, but Idlewood is not a normal house," Emily said.

Anna laughed. "Trust me, I've noticed."

"Oh." Emily looked surprised. So did Charlie.

"Really?" he asked.

Did they really think she was that stupid? Anna raised her arms. "It's obvious to anyone who looks. Why do you think I've been so eager to explore it?"

"Not that obvious," Charlie muttered. "The grown-ups haven't noticed. But I guess they haven't been where you've been." He smiled at Anna, an odd expression on his face.

Oh, this again. "What?" Anna asked, folding her arms.

"*Anyway*, it turns out there are codes in the walls," Emily said, taking back the conversation. "One of them is here."

"Codes?" Anna stepped up beside Emily and looked

at the painting. Bamboo stalks—that was all she saw. But to Emily and Charlie, they must mean something else. "What do they say?"

"They lead to treasure," Charlie said. "We're going to need to write these down again. I'll go get a pen and paper." He raced out.

Anna's eyes widened. "Treasure?" Virginia's treasure, maybe?

But Emily shook her head. "We don't know that. Personally, I think the message is some secret Elaine left behind for someone to figure out later."

That was even more interesting. Treasure was all well and good, but what might be so important—so secret—that Elaine Gardner had to say it in code?

What if she knew what really happened to Virginia?

Anna's heart started racing. When Charlie returned with a pen and a page torn out of one of his puzzle books, she snatched them from his hands. "Read out the numbers, Emily," she said. "I'll write them down. It will be faster this way."

"Well, excuse you," Charlie mumbled, but he didn't fight her.

"Huh? Okay. They're in sets of three. The first one: one, one, six," Emily said, then moved on to the next panel.

Anna jotted down the numbers as fast as Emily read them aloud. When she had eight sets, Emily said, "That's all."

Charlie hurried over and took the list from Anna. He

pushed his glasses up his nose and leaned over it. Anna watched him. "Does that mean anything to you?" she asked.

He pulled back. "It definitely looks like a book cipher," he said. He turned to Emily. "But yeah, without the book, we can't solve this."

"Book cipher?" Anna asked.

"A code in a book," Emily said. "These numbers tell us how to read it. But we don't have the book."

Ohh. "That's the book that went missing from Charlie!"

Charlie nodded. "Emily found the numbers and I found the book. But someone took both of them from us, which is how I knew it couldn't have been you."

"Thanks, I think." Anna looked at the numbers. So close and yet so far. "How'd you find the book in the first place?"

"Another code. Dorky, I know." He kicked at the carpet.

"No! It got you here!" As Charlie grinned, Anna thought. "The book was *Treasure Island*, right?"

Charlie nodded. "But it might have to be the exact same edition as the one the code was written for. That way the words will be at the right spot on each page. I couldn't find any copies except for the one on the bookcase upstairs, and that was a really old edition."

Wait. A really old copy of *Treasure Island*? That rang a bell. Anna had seen the copy on the bookcase door, but she was certain she had seen another one. An old one, sitting on an old, dusty chair in an old, dusty hallway.

She squealed and jumped up and down. "It wasn't the only copy," she said to a bewildered Charlie and Emily. "Come with me! Hurry!"

Anna raced out of the China suite, Charlie and Emily in hot pursuit. All three came to a breathless halt in front of the bookcase at the end of the hall.

"This is where I found my copy," Charlie said. "I don't think the thief would put it back."

"Anyone think it's weird how we haven't seen any of the adults except that one couple this morning?" Emily asked, but Anna ignored her and yanked on the bookcase.

It didn't budge. Well, that was embarrassing. "This used to be a door," she said. "Now it's sealed. I don't know why."

Emily touched the side. "I believe you. Where did it lead?"

Anna pointed up. "Ever notice how Idlewood has three rows of windows but only two floors?"

"The upstairs." Emily smiled. "Where the Gardners' personal rooms were."

Charlie also grinned. "So that's where you've been running off to every day."

Anna nodded. "There's all kinds of old things up there. Including another copy of *Treasure Island*."

"Which you discovered by exploring. Wow," Charlie said. "Then come on. There's got to be a way to open this." He grabbed both sides of the bookcase and leaned back, pulling with all his might.

"It won't open," Anna said. "I don't know why. But there's another way up."

Charlie let go and fell back. He scrambled to his feet. "Let's go."

"You sure?"

"We both are," Emily said. "Show us the way."

"Okay," Anna said, looking at both of them and landing her gaze on her brother. "I'll take you there, but I warn you, you're not going to like it."

15

"I HATE THIS," Charlie said as the wind whipped through his hair.

"I knew you would," Anna said, looking down. She had gone first, to show him and Emily where the footholds were.

Emily was below Charlie, and Charlie preferred it that way. If he followed Anna, step by step, he'd make it up. And if he fell, well, maybe Emily could stop his fall.

It didn't make logical sense, with gravity and human reflexes and everything, but if imagining Emily catching him if he slipped could trick Charlie's brain into thinking this whole climbing-the-side-of-a-mansion thing was safe, then he wasn't complaining.

"Charlie," Emily called. "That handhold is open."

Charlie took a shuddering breath, closed his eyes briefly to recenter himself, and then snapped them open. He reached with a shaking hand to the next stone. The real trick would be managing to make his feet grip the next foothold without his jellylike knees betraying him.

"You guys didn't have to come up," Anna said, pulling herself up to the next stone. "I could have gone up and gotten the book on my own and brought it back down."

"And miss out on seeing where the Gardners and Virginia Maines lived while they were here?" Emily said. "Not a chance."

Anna had explained everything, how she'd found Virginia's old room in the tower and had been reading her letters. Neither Charlie nor Emily had been particularly surprised, but Emily had started to bounce on her toes when she heard that they were going to the place Virginia Maines had once lived.

Charlie wished he had that kind of enthusiasm for climbing a tower. He pressed himself closer to the wall. When Anna explained they'd need to climb the tower, he should have stayed behind. He could have waited down on the grass for the girls to return with the book.

But if Charlie's parents found him alone without Anna, then his sister would get into trouble because she wasn't supposed to be left alone anymore. And even if that weren't a problem, the book clue was his, from start to finish. He'd started it, and no matter how terrifying it was, he was going to finish it. He had to *know*.

That push, that desire to know more, was more powerful than any fear of heights could ever be.

"Charlie? Do you want to go back down?" Anna was

sitting on a ledge, just a few feet above him. She might as well have been half a mile away.

"Not a chance," he said, and pulled himself up to the ledge.

Anna grabbed his arm and helped him up. She smiled at him, and then, as Charlie rested, she helped guide Emily the rest of the way up. They took a few moments to rest together and then finished the climb.

It helped if Charlie didn't think too much about where he was. He kept his eyes either up, on Anna and the next stone to grab, or straight ahead at the rock in front of him. *Get the book, get the book,* he thought, making a rhythm with the words and the beat of his hands and feet hitting the wall.

Get the book, get the book, don't look down, don't look down . . .

"Hey." It was Anna. She was leaning out a window and had grabbed Charlie's arm. "You're here."

"Oh." Charlie pushed himself over the windowsill as Anna pulled him in. Then he collapsed against the wall in the dusty tower room.

"I didn't know you had it in you," Anna said.

"Me neither," Charlie gasped. Man, his arms ached! And his hands were raw and scratched.

But look how high he'd climbed! He, Charlie Henderson! He'd climbed up a house, up a tower, without a rope or harness or anything.

He was never going to do it again.

"Where's the book?" he asked Anna.

"Emily, up to your right," she called out the window, and then raised a hand to Charlie. "Wait a moment."

So Charlie waited for a small eternity until Emily climbed up over the sill, wondering what was happening with the adults downstairs. It had been easy for the kids to escape the house unnoticed. The parlor had been full of the adults, all shouting, with Mr. Llewellyn shouting the loudest of all: "QUIET DOWN! EVERYONE! WE HAVE TO GET TO THE BOTTOM OF THIS!"

To the bottom of what? Had the grown-ups discovered the puzzles in the house and launched their own investigations? Had Mr. Argent found the treasure with his metal detector? Or had the thief gotten to it first? Were they too late?

Emily thumped into the room, shaking Charlie out of his thoughts. "That's . . . a lot higher . . . than it looked," she wheezed, crouching down, elbows on her knees. Then she looked around at the tower room and instantly seemed to get her energy back.

"All this time," Emily said, "this was right over our heads." She let out a shriek and jumped up and down. "Look! These were Virginia's travel charts and maps. And that was her bed! It looks like it hasn't been touched since she vanished." Emily leaned over the dusty comforter.

Charlie looked around the little room. It was kind of cool. Like stepping back in time, in a way. Too bad the layers of dust ruined the effect.

"I found these letters," Anna said, touching a stack of envelopes on the desk. "From Elaine to Virginia."

Emily froze, staring at Anna. "Are you serious?"

Anna nodded. "And Virginia's journal was hidden here, too. See?" She pointed at an old, ragged leather book.

"But you *found it*?" Emily raced over to Anna and the desk. "Oh my gosh, I have to read them. Who knows what kind of amazing stories are inside, lost to the ages—"

Charlie coughed, partly from the dust but also to interrupt Emily. "Maybe you read the journal later?"

The girls nodded, though Emily tucked the journal under her arm.

"The other copy of the book is this way," Anna said, pointing down a set of spiral stairs. "In the main hallway. Let's go."

What Charlie had taken for a small tower room was actually much larger. The stairs snaking down it were crossed with ropes and swings, and lined with books and more maps and charts, and once they reached the bottom, there were couches and chairs. Virginia must have had a great living area here for when she planned her next adventure. Charlie could almost see her, surrounded by charts, plotting her journeys, marking a new route.

Here there was no gold, no silver, no treasure. Virginia had vanished and taken nothing with her, but if the treasure wasn't in her room, then it must be hidden *somewhere*. The code would have to show them where.

The climb down to the main hallway was much easier than the climb up the tower. Anna pointed out the sneaky entrance to the tower, but when she tried the tower's normal third-floor door from the inside, it opened, so they used that.

The three entered a hallway that looked like something out of a horror movie. The emptiness, with the gray film of dust everywhere, made the rooms look old and faded, as transparent as ghosts.

"There are the steps to the bookcase door," Anna said, pointing.

Charlie shivered. That moment when the bookcase shook. Now that he knew where his sister had been escaping to, he was sure it must have been her, doing something to shake the hidden door. But, still, there had been that howl he heard just afterward.

If there was no ghost, what could have howled like that?

Anna stopped and picked up a torn book. "Here it is," she said. "Is this the right edition?"

Charlie took the book, with Emily peering over his shoulder. "It's a little ratty," he said. "The cover's missing. But I'm pretty sure it's the same edition as the one I lost."

"Then what are we waiting for?" Emily asked. "Let's solve the code."

She pulled out the list of numbers, and Charlie opened the book. "What's the first set?" he asked.

"One, one, six," Emily read, and Charlie turned to the first page, down to the first line, and read the sixth word out loud.

"The."

"The," Anna repeated, eyes closed.

"Keep going," Charlie said.

Emily read out each set, and Charlie flipped through the book until he found every one.

Unfortunately, it made a bunch of gibberish, when it worked at all. Some of the last numbers were huge, way too big for a single line of text. Charlie had been trying the edition-sensitive "page, line, word in that line" method, but it led to nothing. With the girls staring at him, he muttered, "Must be 'chapter, paragraph, word,'" and started again. So, they didn't need the exact edition. Whatever. They still needed the book, and it wasn't too hard to redo the code.

Fortunately, the first word was the same. And, this time, it made sense.

"The."

"Door."

"Was."

"Open."

"Between."

"The."

"Dragon."

"Wings. And that's it," Charlie said, closing the book.

"The door was open between the dragon wings," Anna said.

"The door was . . . I'm sorry, I have no idea what it means," Emily said.

"We're looking for a door?" Charlie asked. "That's what I'm getting. Are you sure that was the whole message?"

"That was every set of numbers in those paintings," Emily said. "I don't know if there were other paintings like that in your suite, but I'm guessing there weren't. And are you sure you got the whole message from the Rome wall?"

"I've heard this message before," Anna was muttering, eyes still closed. "Where have I heard it before?"

"I'm sure. Dragon wings," Charlie said. "*Dragon wings.* The door must be marked with dragons."

"Yes!" Emily said. "But which ones? There are so many dragons in Idlewood. All the ones in the China suite, for example."

"Between the dragon wings," Anna said again, opening her eyes.

Emily snapped her fingers. "The downstairs hall," she said. "Those two big dragon statues!"

"They're on either side of that carved door!" Charlie said.

"But they weren't earlier! Someone moved one."

Charlie grinned. "That has to be it."

"No," Anna said. "It's not. Can I see the journal?"

Emily handed Virginia's journal over and Anna flipped back and forth through the pages. "I knew that sentence sounded familiar," she said. "There's this story in here about Ginny jumping out of her plane over the Amazon jungle."

"Ginny?" Charlie asked.

"Jumping out of a plane?" Emily looked over Anna's shoulder. "I've never heard that story."

"Neither had I. I think Ginny kept it to herself. Here it is." Anna stopped and read aloud, "'The door was open between the dragon's wings, and I soon grew wings of my own as the green jungle rushed up to meet me.'"

"That's the line," Charlie said. "Or close enough."

"But it's not about China or dragon statues," Anna said. "She was in her plane."

Emily's eyes widened, and Charlie felt the realization hit him like a freight train. "Her plane's name was the *Dragon*," he whispered.

Anna snapped the journal closed. Her eyes blazed. "I know where the treasure is," she said.

16

THE CLIMB BACK down the tower was even trickier than the one up. Anna went down before Charlie, pointing out handholds. It was slow going; all those years of sitting around, reading instead of playing outside, had caught up to him. Maybe Anna should have invited him out more often. She just never thought he'd come with her. Watching him puff and tremble but still climb the tower had proved her wrong. Maybe he did care about things outside his books.

Emily was struggling to climb down, too. She'd taken Virginia's journal and was balancing that on her way down the wall. Anna sighed. This was why she never brought anything down with her. And the fact that it was stealing.

"Borrowing," Emily had called it. "We might need the journal later. We'll put it back."

Anna had no response to that, other than to suggest they hurry.

When they reached the grass, Charlie dropped to the ground and hugged it. "I hope someone got a picture of that, because I'm never doing it again," he said. "Never, ever again."

"Get up," Anna said, smiling. "It wasn't that bad."

"Maybe not for you," he said. But he was also smiling when he stood. "Okay. Take us to the door."

"This way. It's on the second floor." Anna took off, and Emily and Charlie ran after her.

When they stepped through the front doors, they stopped short.

Idlewood, usually so quiet in the morning, had turned into a madhouse. Mr. Mustache was yelling at Mr. Llewellyn, who was trying to calm him down but whose own face had turned as red as his tie for today.

"I understand wanting to stop thieves, but this search is too much," Mr. Mustache was saying. "My wife is easily exhausted! She's taking a quiet stroll on the grounds to calm down, but I don't think we can stay here another night."

Book Lady, hair loose, had dragged her suitcase downstairs and had it open on the carpet. Piles of books, titled everything from *Spaghetti in Space* to *How to Pan for Gold*, spilled out. "There," she said. "I have nothing to hide."

"Nor do I," Suitcase Man said, one of his hands resting on Braid Lady's arm. A metal detector hung from his other hand, and his pinned suitcase lay open in front of him. Behind them, Garrett and the cook were dragging one of the dragon statues across the hall. Garrett was chatting with the cook the whole time. "I can't believe they thought a tarp would hide this. Seriously, it was the first place I looked. Where was it supposed to go, again? By the door? That makes sense. The other dragon looks just like it . . ." He was still talking after they placed the statue by the carved door and left the hall.

"What's going on?" Charlie asked the others.

"No idea," Emily said. She glanced at Anna.

"What? I had nothing to do with this," Anna said.

"For once," Charlie added, and Anna shoved him.

Emily's parents passed by, and when they spotted her, they rushed over. "Where have you been?" they asked. "Why are you covered in dust?"

"Just exploring with Charlie and Anna," Emily said. Anna noticed her quietly slide the journal behind her. "What's happening?"

Emily's mom and dad passed a glance between them. "Rosie and Xavier were caught stealing the antiques in the house," she said.

"No!"

Emily's mom nodded. "They took an old dictionary, one of the dragon statues from the lobby, and lots of smaller items. Garrett and his mother are handling the police and putting the antiques back where they belong."

"His mother?"

"The cook. They're having a time of it, apparently.

The Arctic Circle suite is littered with stolen things. Garrett said they found a crystal clock tucked under the stuffed penguin like an egg."

Emily snorted. "A penguin in the Arctic? That doesn't fit. I bet they stole that, too."

"Perhaps. But now everyone is throwing accusations left and right, and we're all supposed to open our doors and be ready to be searched. No one is allowed to go out onto the grounds."

Rosie and Xavier? They didn't seem like thieves, but then, who did? It wasn't like Anna had been around, watching the guests the whole weekend.

But if they'd been secret thieves, and the Shaughnessys secret historians, who else might have come here with a secret motive? Suitcase Man had been holding a metal detector. The Sunglasses Couple ran off as often as Anna did, and sometimes, they smelled a little musty. Who was the treasure hunter who had stolen Emily's and Charlie's codes?

Emily's dad looked at the kids. "If I were you, I'd stay out of everyone's way. Tensions are high enough as it is right now."

Charlie nodded, as did Emily. Anna just smiled. "That's the plan," she said.

Emily's parents left, heading back upstairs, apparently to participate in the search. Anna turned to Emily. "Why didn't you show them the journal?"

"Not now! Not when everyone is freaking out about thieves stealing from the house. And we're not done yet.

We don't know *why* the codes were left. So," Emily said. "The door?"

"Second floor," Anna repeated. "Come on."

The three went upstairs as quickly and quietly as they could as Anna led them into the heart of the ongoing search for thieves.

◆ ◆ ◆

On the second floor they passed angry adults slamming doors and nervous adults welcoming in Mr. Llewellyn, big-eared and big-mouthed Garrett, and the sharp-faced cook. Emily pulled her hair in front of her face, playing the shy, invisible kid once again.

But who was she kidding? She was following public enemy number one (who also had bright red hair) down the line of suites, and stopping in front of one.

Its door was closed. Anna reached out to open it but hesitated.

"Why are you stopping?" Emily asked.

"This is where I got caught earlier," Anna said. "You know, Emily, you don't need to keep coming with me. Show your parents the upstairs rooms and the journal. That will be enough to prove there's more to this house."

Emily had considered that. But she couldn't stop now. They were neck-deep in a mystery, history in the making, and she was part of it! Stopping now would be worse than walking out of a movie halfway through. Emily needed to be there when this story ended.

But what if it already had? Why was the door closed? Could whoever had stolen Charlie's book and Emily's numbers already be inside, opening the door to the treasure? What if they'd already found it? Emily couldn't let that happen.

Pushing past Anna, she knocked on the door. "Open up! We have to search everyone!" She twisted the doorknob.

It turned easily. The door was unlocked, and when the kids stepped inside, it was empty.

"Hello?" Emily called. "Anyone home?"

"Could you keep it down?" Charlie asked. "What if Mr. Llewellyn hears us?"

"No one's here," Emily said, ignoring him. She looked around the room. "Wow."

"I know," Anna said.

Emily hadn't been able to see this room. The guests here had been out whenever she thought about stopping by. But it was fascinating. Painted gray like the metal of an airplane, a cockpit of sorts filled one corner. In the walls were painted windows showing the ocean beneath the fake plane, and painted on the back wall was the airplane's door.

"That's it," Emily and Anna said at the same time. They approached the door.

Charlie hung back. "I'll be lookout," he said. "Tell me if you find anything."

"Lookout?" Emily asked as Charlie pushed up his glasses and turned his attention to the hall.

"Makes sense. Where are the guests?" Anna responded.

"Mr. Haskell's in the entry hall. I don't know about his wife," Emily said. "I think . . . I think I've seen her around."

"Where?"

Frowning, Emily thought back to when she and Charlie had been talking. "I might be wrong, but . . . I saw this woman examining the lock at the carved door downstairs."

"Are you sure it wasn't one of the women staying in the Egypt room?"

Emily shook her head. "Not at first. But then I saw her today with Mr. Haskell, and she dropped her key. She's . . . rather short when she hunches over."

Charlie peeked into the room. "The lady with the curly gray hair?"

"And the big quilted bag?" Anna said.

"That's her!" Emily had the picture in her head: Mrs. Haskell. Tall, but sometimes short. Gray-haired. Carried a quilted bag. All of them, the same person.

"I saw her in the parlor, searching under the sofa." Charlie made a face. "It's weird. I keep seeing her in this hallway. I saw her right before my book went missing."

Emily stiffened. She'd seen the woman leave and come back during the old-fashioned night, grinning like a well-fed cat and clutching that big quilted bag. What could fit in that bag under all the candy she was always passing out to the kids? An old book? A set of code numbers?

Anna was eyeing them. "You think Mrs. Haskell is the one who stole your stuff?"

It sounded weird, saying it out loud, so Emily started to shake her head but then said, "Maybe. I don't know."

"She was in the maze," Charlie said. "When I was talking about book codes. She could have heard me."

"I don't doubt you," Anna said, raising her hands. "The Haskells were talking with my parents, and it sounds like they travel a lot. They said they win trips, but no one can be that lucky, right? You're different," she added, as Charlie was about to pipe up.

Emily realized she was clenching her fists. Why hadn't she seen it before? Every time she saw Mrs. Haskell, she was poking around the house. Just like Emily had been.

"And she was looking at a lock," Emily said through gritted teeth. "Someone snuck into my family's suite and yours to steal our things. Maybe someone with experience picking locks?"

It made sense. It *all* made sense.

"Anyway," Anna continued, "didn't her husband say she was on the grounds? We were just out there. *High* up there. How come we didn't see her?" She gestured around. "Plus, this is the Haskells' room. If Mrs. Haskell is our thief, and she's searching for whatever Elaine left behind, and the door is in here—"

"Right. Let's get to work." Charlie turned back to watch the hall.

Anna was right. Mrs. Haskell could be there already,

taking the treasure or message or whatever it was and leaving Emily with *nothing* to prove that the codes had any real meaning.

Emily touched the painted airplane door with shaking fingers. "This wasn't here in the old days," she said.

"The room? Or the door?" Anna had dropped to her knees and was feeling around the baseboard.

"Both. The rooms were decorated like this for the guests by order of Elaine Gardner, using items left in Idlewood by the family. The family didn't live in themed suites, after all. These painted walls could have a clue hidden in them, like the ones in Rome and China. And if this is the door—"

"Between the dragon's wings," Anna finished. "It must be. I just don't know what we're looking for around it."

She had a point. Emily couldn't see any letters, numbers, or patterns, nothing that screamed "CODE!" to her. It made sense that this would be the most difficult code yet, but she couldn't even determine where to start.

"Charlie might know," Emily said. "Hey, Charlie! Get in here!"

Charlie poked his head in. "Just a moment!" he hissed, and a second later, Emily heard him say, loudly, "Hi, Mr. Llewellyn!"

"Drop!" Anna said, and both girls crouched, breathing heavily.

Outside the door, Mr. Llewellyn and Charlie were talking. Anna was pressed against the painted door.

Emily squeezed her nails into her palms. *Don't come in, don't come in.*

After what seemed like hours, Charlie whispered, "All clear."

Emily slumped. "Whew. I thought it was over."

"Not yet," Charlie said. "But the hall is packed. I don't know how we're going to get out of here when we're done."

"We'll go out through here." Anna was running one hand up and down along the edge of the airplane door. "There's a seam in the wall."

Charlie rushed in. "Let me see!"

Emily and Charlie pushed Anna aside to feel the wall. She'd been right. Beneath Emily's fingertips was a thin, but very real, crack in the wall. It went all around the painted door's edge.

"So it is a door," Emily said. "It's not a code. It's a real door!"

"Yeah, but how do we open it?" Anna asked.

"How did you open the door to the upstairs?"

"No idea. It just opened. Wait." Anna fumbled in her pocket and fished out the tarnished key. Emily reached for it, and Anna pulled it away. "I found this near the house," she said. "Maybe it unlocks the door."

"I don't see a keyhole," Emily said. "Maybe it's hidden?"

Without a word, Anna started feeling the wall, and Emily did the same. The secret had to be here somewhere.

◆ ◆ ◆

As the girls searched the wall, Charlie dropped to the ground. The baseboard was interesting, with painted dragons swirling around each other. Maybe they spelled out a code or message on how to open the door?

Charlie glanced at the front door to the suite, now closed. Where were the Haskells? If Mrs. Haskell was the one who'd taken his book, then she (and maybe her husband, too) could have solved the puzzle and were ahead of them. And either of them could walk in at any second and see three kids fiddling with their wall—one of whom (Anna) was doing her level best to physically pull it apart at the seams.

Who would have thought Anna would be the one to find the answer to the code? This room and this door? Charlie had always thought she didn't care about anything cerebral, but clearly, in Anna's exploring, there was more going on under that mass of red hair than he'd thought.

He examined the dragon paintings. They were small, thin images, swirling and dancing around each other like dragons in flight. Very pretty. But was there a pattern?

Not one Charlie could see. Three would be pointed right, then two left, then one up and one down, but the pattern didn't repeat itself. Then Charlie noticed, leaning closer to the space just to the right of the door, that there was a segment where three rows of three dragons faced right, one swirled, chasing its own tail, and three sets of three faced left.

Like arrows, pointing at the one in the middle. Why would they do that?

As Anna and Emily debated the merits of finding a crowbar, Charlie touched the circular center dragon. It was slightly raised. He gave it a firm push.

Behind the wall, ancient machinery creaked and squealed. Both girls jumped back. And the painted door swung open as far as its rusty hinges would allow.

Anna pried the door farther open, and the three kids looked inside. There was a hall, or rather, a secret passage. Bare boards lined the walls, and support beams were clearly visible. Dust, dead bugs, and mouse droppings lined the ground.

"Oh my gosh," Emily said. She pushed past Anna and stepped into the hall. Under her feet, the dust puffed up in a small cloud. "How long has this been here?"

"Probably since Elaine renovated the house," Charlie said. This was way more than a couple of neatly painted letters on a wall—the foreman Silver must have been in on the scheme, to build a tunnel like this. So many years ago . . . had he used workers to build it? Did they tell their families?

"Think Mrs. Haskell is ahead of us?" Emily asked.

"We'd see footprints in the dust," Anna said. She stepped into the hall after Emily.

Charlie followed them, scuffing the dust with his sneaker. Beneath his shoe, he could see another set of footprints. And another. Faint but there. The Haskells? Or old footprints, left protected by time? "Like these?" he said, pointing.

"But the door was closed," Emily said.

"So was the door to the plane room," Anna said. "If I

were being sneaky, I wouldn't want anyone wondering, 'Hey, why is that door-that's-not-supposed-to-be-a-door open?' And," she said, scuffing her feet and erasing a footprint, "this was an old door. Don't you think it opened just a little too easily?"

Emily grimaced. "Let's go," she said, striding down the dim passage. "We are *not* too late. We can't be. I won't let us lose."

17

THE HALL was dark, lit only by the light from the room behind them, but Emily didn't care. She forged ahead, Anna hurrying beside her and Charlie just behind. There was no way Mrs. Haskell had found the treasure before her. No way. *No way.*

She had not climbed a freaking wall, borrowed an old journal (which was still under her arm), and broken into a guest's room to find out that the ending of this story was a big fat nothing. Elaine had left a message, and Emily had solved it. The truth, the treasure, all of it . . . it was meant for *her.*

And, well, Anna and Charlie. As much as Emily had worked for this, she had to admit she could never have solved the whole mystery without Charlie's code-solving and Anna's discovery of the tower room and journal. *The door between the dragon's wings.* Even if she'd found that clue alone, Emily might have gone to the carved door in the entry hall instead of this one.

The passage turned a corner and the light faded even more. Emily could see a set of stairs ahead, and warned the others.

"Be careful not to trip," Anna said.

Keeping one hand on the wall, Emily climbed the stairs. So many years. Were they even safe to step on anymore?

Either way, Emily kept going, as did the Hendersons. Soon, they reached a top landing.

"I think we're back on the third floor," Anna whispered.

"I think you're right," Emily whispered back. She stepped forward and walked into a closed door, banging her forehead.

"You found it," Charlie said, and Emily, rubbing her head, glared in the direction of his voice.

Emily reached out and felt a door beneath her hands. "I think I did."

"Let me see." Anna put a hand on Emily's shoulder and reached out to the door. "I feel a knob and a keyhole," she said. "What if . . ."

There was a short moment of shuffling, and then the sound of metal scratching against metal. "Doesn't fit," she said, stepping back.

Hmm. Well, what if . . . Emily grabbed the doorknob and twisted it. It opened easily.

"Not locked," she said.

"Not good," Charlie said. "Of course the door would be unlocked if someone beat us to the treasure."

"Then let's stop hanging around here." Emily pushed the door open, and light flooded the dark hallway.

All three of them shoved their way inside the next room and stopped. Emily wasn't sure what she'd been expecting, but the confused frown on Charlie's face mirrored her own feelings.

They'd stepped into a small, unfinished room, probably crammed between two of the main rooms on the third floor. One single window illuminated the scene, sending shafts of sunlight through the swirling dust.

But other than the dust, the room was empty—all but a drawer-less wooden table pushed up against the window.

"Where's the treasure?" Charlie asked.

"We were too late," Anna said. "Mrs. Haskell must have already come and cleared it out. Maybe she did it right after stealing your code."

Emily just shook her head. They couldn't have lost. Elaine had given her the clues, and they'd made it here together. Some cheating treasure hunter couldn't have taken it all. Now Emily wouldn't have the treasure, and she'd never know what Elaine's message had been. She'd have to live her whole life not knowing.

Anna was shaking her head. "No, wait. It can't be that easy."

Charlie kicked at a lump of dust. "I missed the part where any of this was easy."

"No, I mean . . . up in the tower, when I picked up the journal, it left behind a clean spot," Anna said. "Where the dust landed on the journal but not the floor underneath. So where are the clean spots?"

Emily felt like she suddenly remembered it was her birthday. "There aren't any. Nothing was taken from here recently!"

"So whatever was left is still here," Charlie said. "We can still find it. Clever catch, Anna!"

Anna twisted a loose curl, and Emily waved around the room. "Search everywhere."

The three scattered, checking the walls for hidden compartments or cracks. Emily ran her hands over the splintery wood, searching for seams. Nothing.

But what if it wasn't in the walls? That table by the window. Emily turned around and saw Anna and Charlie also staring at the table.

"It's the only furniture in here," Anna said.

"But it doesn't have any drawers," Charlie said.

"Doesn't mean that's not it," Emily added.

They stood silently for a couple of seconds, and then, all at once, approached the table. Anna dropped to the ground, scooting under the table like she was a mechanic and it was a car.

"I see something," she said.

Emily resisted the urge to drop and look, too. Anna would have it out in a moment, and a second person under there would only slow her down. But it was *agonizing*.

A minute later, Anna's hand popped out, holding a box. "Got it!"

Emily took the box and set it on the table. It was wooden, fastened only with a twine tie wrapped around it. She wriggled the string, pushing it off the edge of the box.

"It was stuck to the bottom of the table," Anna said, standing up. Her hair was ashen with dust. Emily suddenly understood why she was always showing up with wet hair. "There were latches down there holding it in place."

Charlie was hopping around. "What's inside? Do you think it's money? Or jewels? Hey, Anna, what treasures did Virginia bring back? What would be inside?"

"Shhh!" Emily batted Charlie away. She took a deep breath and opened the box.

Inside lay the torn-off cover of a book. Emily laughed, pulling it out. "Our good friend *Treasure Island*," she said, showing the others.

Charlie laughed, too, and took it before passing it to Anna. She tossed her hair, sending up a cloud of dust, and examined the cover, smiling at a doodle of a tree house scribbled on the back.

"What else is in there?" Charlie asked, leaning over. "A book?"

"Yeah." Emily pulled it out. The book, bound in green leather, was heavy and large, with wide pages. A red ribbon marked a page, so she opened to it.

There was a piece of paper folded and stuck between the pages. Emily removed it, setting it aside to reveal rows of numbers underneath, but on the left side were words. "Gold Celtic . . . bracelet," Emily read out loud, struggling with the old handwriting. "Wooden mask."

Anna gasped and set the *Treasure Island* book cover on the table. "The ledger," she said.

Emily frowned. "How did you know about the ledger?"

"I . . . I read the paper you had jammed in your book," Anna said. "I'm sorry."

"It's okay," Emily said. "I might have done the same thing. So you know about the scandal, then."

Anna nodded. "Virginia apparently sold her treasures, including a Buddha statue, to the Mob, and then she vanished. Does Charlie know?"

"He does," Charlie said.

"Don't tell anyone about the letter," Emily said. "My parents thought it was great, but they couldn't verify anything he said. With memories that old, it could just be stories told to a child, remembered poorly. Mom and Dad couldn't do anything about it without a second witness."

"Well, you have one now," Anna said, pointing to the ledger.

Emily nodded and continued scanning the list, then stopped. "Jade Buddha," she read. "That was the last treasure the Mob got. So was this what Elaine was hiding? Proof that Virginia had been involved with the Mob?"

"That doesn't make any sense," Charlie said. He traced the lines of numbers. "I mean, it was a big deal to the Gardners, right? Why hide the proof instead of destroying it?"

"Yeah," Emily said. It was odd. Simon Gardner's letter said that the family did all they could to hide the truth. Even his sisters didn't know anything. So why would Elaine rig elaborate clues to lead to this ledger instead of tossing it in the massive fireplace downstairs? Why require that the house remain unchanged so the clues would be there long after the Gardners left?

"This isn't the proof," Anna said. "I found *that* evidence upstairs in Ginny's room. If Elaine was trying to hide the ledger, why leave pages up there? And," she said, eyes widening as she looked at the ledger in Emily's hands, "that's not Ginny's handwriting."

"Oh. *Oh.*" Emily set the ledger down and pulled out Virginia's journal. Opening to a random page, she set it beside the rows of items sold to the Mob.

"They're different," she said. "Virginia's handwriting leans right. This stands straight up."

That wasn't the only difference. As Emily compared the two, she could see how Virginia's letters were small and quick, and these were large and loopy. Her heart raced. If she was right, this was the reason for the clues, for the house's unchanged status. And she was holding the proof in her hands.

But why would Elaine keep this information secret for so long? She loved her sister. Why not just tell the police that Virginia was innocent and she could prove it? And if Virginia didn't sell her treasures to the Mob, who did?

"So if this isn't Virginia's handwriting," Emily asked out loud, "then whose is it?"

"Um, I think this might help us," Charlie said. He held up the paper that had been stuck in the ledger. "I mean, it was in the book for a reason, right?"

"Let me see." Emily took it and unfolded it, and she, Anna, and Charlie huddled to read it.

It was a letter from Everett Gardner to Elaine. "'My dear,'" Emily read. "'Happy birthday! I'm afraid that if you want your present, you will have to work for it: 7-15 6-9-18-19-20 20-15 20-8-5 13-1-26-5 1-14-4 19-5-5-11 20-8-5 3-5-14-20-5-18.'"

A simple birthday note from husband to wife. But Emily started tapping the paper, hard. The handwriting was large and loopy. It stood straight up.

It was a match for the handwriting in the ledger.

"It was Everett," Anna said. She slammed a fist down on the table. "He was the one who was selling Ginny's gifts to the Mob!"

"But why?" Charlie asked. "Weren't the Gardners rich?"

"They were, but they had some trouble once," Anna said. "In the letters, Elaine mentioned not having enough money. Everett often complained about financial troubles, and he worked a lot. And then the comments stopped. Elaine would mention how the things Ginny brought for them went missing. Turns out it was her husband selling them the whole time. And he framed Ginny for it."

"Look," Charlie said, pointing at the bottom of the note.

A message, in a different handwriting, lay under the numbers. *R'n hliib*.

"That's Atbash," he said. "A equals Z, and R equals I. You can tell because the R is alone, and I is the only letter in the English language that's set apart like that."

"So what does it say, genius?" Anna asked.

"'I'm sorry.'" Charlie stepped back. "That's what it says."

"You can decode that fast?"

Charlie took off his glasses to clean away the dust. "I can if it's Atbash. I'm practically fluent by now."

"You nerd."

As the Hendersons bickered, each wearing a smile, Emily read the note again. *I'm sorry.* A note from Elaine to Virginia.

She must have found out after her sister disappeared. They'd fought, Virginia had vanished, and then Elaine found out Everett was the criminal. How must that have felt? Everett was also a loving husband. They had three kids, and from all records, he cared about them all. What could have made him go so far, and how had Elaine reacted?

By telling the truth, the only way she could. She needed to tell her sister that she knew Virginia was innocent, but she didn't want to incriminate Everett, either. So she left the clues behind, a way of telling the truth without hurting more people she loved.

But had anyone but Anna, Charlie, and Emily ever received the message? The box looked like it had been left under the table, unmoved, since Elaine put it there. And what had happened to Virginia? Would anyone ever know more than just a *part* of the mystery?

But that part was enough for Emily, and enough for Idlewood. Emily put the note inside the ledger and closed it. Then she set Virginia's journal on top and picked up the stack.

"Come on," she said. "Let's get this back to my parents and Mr. Llewellyn."

"We can't leave!" Anna said. "I want to know what happened to Virginia! So we know she was innocent. That doesn't explain how she disappeared without a trace and how no one ever found any sign of her again. Do you think Everett *made* her vanish so no one would ever find out he was the crook?"

Charlie gave a freaked-out look to his sister. "You think he would?"

"After all this, it wouldn't surprise me."

Emily shook her head. It wouldn't surprise her, either, but she didn't think Everett had done it. The forged ledger had been enough to convince the police, and Virginia never went to court. He'd been safe. He never knew that someone else discovered his secret, and even if he did, Everett wouldn't have harmed his family. Emily said as much to Anna and Charlie.

"But he got away with it!" Anna said.

"Not really." Emily grinned. "Elaine found out, and,

well, maybe karma got him. Everett Gardner was killed by a mountain lion."

"Oh. That's . . . better. But still, we can't give it up now," Anna said. "There's more to the mystery."

Emily sighed. "I know. But maybe there are some mysteries that aren't meant to be solved. Maybe, no matter how much we look and try, we need to let them go." She held up the books. "We solved a decades-old mystery today and cleared an innocent woman's name. Isn't that enough?"

Anna shuffled her feet, avoiding Emily's eyes. She was disappointed, and to some extent, so was Emily. Her visions of dazzling her parents and Mr. Llewellyn with handfuls of treasure and a map leading to Virginia's hide-outs had gone up in smoke. But in their place was the prospect of showing them the ledger and explaining the clues and how they'd solved them—proof that Elaine had a reason for leaving the house the way it was, that Virginia had, in fact, lived here, and that she was innocent of all charges brought against her.

As she pictured that, Emily felt a pang of anxiety (she was going to get in so much trouble) along with a growing thrill. Maybe she hadn't solved the whole problem, but she *had* solved enough.

The truth of Virginia Maines's so-called Mob connections was a mystery that no one had been able to solve, and the answer had been written in the walls. Emily grinned. If that couldn't save those walls from being torn down, then nothing could.

18

"**COME ON,**" Emily said. "We can't wait around all day!" She started toward the door, ledger book and journal in her arms. Anna followed her.

But Charlie didn't. Something didn't add up. Something was bothering him. Pieces of information, some unwritten code, swirled in his head. The ledger, the missing treasure, an order to never change the house, stolen objects returned to their exact location, and an image of a penguin in the Arctic Circle.

"Wait," he said, and the girls stopped.

"Charlie?" Anna asked. "What's up?"

Charlie waved for the ledger, and Emily handed it back. He opened it to the last page. "Is this complete?" he asked.

The girls stepped forward. "What do you mean?" Emily asked, bending over the page.

"Is it complete? Is this a complete list of everything Virginia brought back? Or are there things missing?"

Anna scanned the ledger. "Things are missing," she said. She gestured at the ledger. "From what I read in the letters, these are mostly just things Ginny gave to the Gardners. Some of them were items she wanted to keep for herself, but I remember other things she kept. Jars of shells, macaw feathers, a statue of Athena . . ."

"Athena?" Emily perked up. "Not Minerva? Athena?"

Anna answered by pulling a picture out of the journal and handing it to Emily. Charlie peered over the girls' shoulders. It was Virginia Maines, standing next to a marble statue. "That's it," Emily said. "Right down to the pose and the gash cutting across her shoulder. It's the same one as the one in our suite."

"Ginny said it was a gift from her Greek friends. Apparently it reminded them of her," Anna said with a laugh. "It was in the letters."

"Let me see that," Charlie said, reaching for the journal. He flipped through it until he found an entry about a penguin. "It says here that there was a penguin that was a favorite of Ginny's," Charlie said. "He would follow her around on her trip to the South Pole, and she fed him fish. When he died, she had him stuffed so she could remember him. There wasn't room in the plane, so she had to take a boat back."

Anna nodded. "I read that story. Bradley wasn't happy."

"I bet that's the penguin in the Arctic Circle suite," Charlie said. His mind hummed. "Why demand that a house stay the same? *Exactly* the same. Sure, to protect the secret passages, and the codes, but what if it was also to keep Virginia's treasures safe?" He shook his head. "'They are safe.' Elaine made sure of it with her order."

The treasures. They were here—they had always been here. But they weren't the kind of things that Mr. Argent would find with his metal detector, not gold and silver. They were *memories*. Stories.

That was what had mattered to Virginia. Charlie looked at the ledger again. All that gold, she'd just given away. She'd kept the gifts and discoveries that reminded her of her adventures and the people she met along the way.

"They're all over the house, I bet," he said. "Virginia's treasures. We could probably find them all."

Emily turned dust pale. "If that's true, then we have so much more than I thought! The codes and mystery could save Idlewood, but if all these old rooms are full of Virginia Maines's missing treasures—not gold and jewels but mementoes with stories behind every single one—then no one could tear this place down!" She snapped up the ledger again. "We have to go. Right now. We have to tell someone before another minute passes!"

Emily took off back down the dark hallway, carrying both ledger and journal. Anna turned to follow her, then stopped and grinned at Charlie. "Treasure, everywhere. Hey, maybe, when they turn this place into a museum, you can have your name listed on the little placards as the guy who discovered them all."

"Oh, I don't know," Charlie said. He took off his glasses and wiped the dust off on his shirt. "Elaine. Virginia. All of this. We couldn't have done it without you."

"Sure you could," Anna said.

"I don't think so," Charlie said. "You're the one who found the journal and knew everything about Virginia, you're the one who kept finding the hidden doors, and you're the one who realized nothing had been taken from the treasure room. Even if no one stole our codes, we'd still be searching for the door between the dragon's wings if it wasn't for you."

Anna smiled. "I was just doing what I always do. Getting into places I'm not supposed to be."

"It was exactly what you were supposed to do," Charlie said. He started moving down the hall, and Anna followed. "You found so much. What did I do but sit around reading codes?"

"Codes? *Codes?* Charlie, *all of this* depended on codes. And you solved them. All of them!"

"Me and Emily."

"Emily found part of the code. But you're the one who understood it *was* a code. You solved it, and you found your way into this room. You're the one who figured out what happened to the treasure. Emily is running back to her parents to report, all thanks to you and your codes."

Charlie grinned. The empty feeling had been replaced with warmth. He'd never heard Anna praise him like this, and it was like magic. Like an adventure from a book.

"I was just doing what I always do," Charlie said.

"Please. You climbed a tower," Anna said. "Both

up and down. All the way to the third floor and back. You're braver than you give yourself credit for. You always have been."

He *had* climbed that tower, hadn't he? Of his own free will. Here, in the dark and dust, safe on firm boards, it was hard to believe. But he had done it.

"I just had to know," Charlie said.

"I understand."

And without another word, Charlie knew she did. Hidden attics and books, wild forests and codes. They really weren't that different: Both contained secrets to be discovered. Anna preferred one and Charlie another, but in the end, they were really after the same thing.

"Hey," Anna said, putting her hand on Charlie's shoulder and squeezing lightly. "This was fun."

"Yeah. And we did it." Charlie turned around and hugged Anna. He hadn't done that since he was six years old, and for a moment, brother and sister held their grip on each other.

After a moment, Anna pushed him away. "We're missing Emily's reveal."

"Let's go."

The siblings hurried down the hallway and back out of the airplane room.

◆ ◆ ◆

Somehow Emily lost the Hendersons, but she knew they'd follow. She slipped out of the secret door and through the Haskells' suite, which was still empty.

In the hall, her parents were talking. "Mom! Dad!" Emily called, carrying the books over.

"Emily! Where were you?" her dad said. "Mr. Llewellyn found pictures all over your bed. What have you been doing?"

Ohh. "Just helping out," Emily said.

"We told you to let us handle this," her mom said. "Mr. Llewellyn doesn't seem very happy. I don't know what he's going to do now."

Emily lifted the books. "Forget the pictures. You have to see this."

"Where did you get those?"

"Anna! Charlie!" It was the Henderson parents seeing their dusty kids, who had emerged from the airplane room. "Where have you been?" Mrs. Henderson said. "Anna, have you been dragging your brother into places you know you're not supposed to be?"

"Why does everyone always assume it's her fault?" Charlie asked. "Maybe it was my idea this time."

Everyone, Emily and parents included, stared at him. "Anyway," Charlie said. "You have to listen to what we found. Emily just saved Idlewood."

Before anyone's parents could say anything, Emily opened up the ledger. She held the note beside the list of items sold and waited for her parents to realize what exactly she held in her arms.

She didn't have to wait long. "Mr. Llewellyn!" her father shouted, taking the book from her. "Mr. Llewellyn, come quick!"

A few moments later, Mr. Llewellyn, breathless, arrived. "What?" he wheezed. He was holding a piece of gold metal in his hand. "I'm sorry, but there's a situation downstairs. Someone picked the lock on the carved door."

The door between the dragon statues. Emily, Charlie, and Anna shared a look. It was the door they'd almost thought was the answer to the code.

"What?" Emily's dad said. "Why?"

Mr. Llewellyn shook his head. "No idea. All that's back there are the gala decorations from when this place hosted big parties and weddings." He held up the gold in his hand. It was a gilded votive candleholder. "All fake and pretty much worthless. But someone has stolen most of it. They left this behind." He held up a hard candy wrapper.

Emily snorted, then bit back the rest of her laughter. The Haskells must have misinterpreted the clue and stolen the wrong treasure! Thank goodness Emily and Charlie had Anna! Judging from the Hendersons' shaking shoulders, they were thinking the same thing.

Mr. Llewellyn turned to the laughing kids and spotted Emily. "You're the girl with all the pictures," he said. "I could believe a child would sneak a phone into Idlewood, but an old Polaroid? And then use it to photograph every room in the house? I can only believe your parents put you up to it."

Emily swallowed. "My parents?"

Mr. Llewellyn faced the Shaughnessys. "I've known who you are since you reserved your spot. Historians with a special interest in saving old houses. I imagine you're trying to save Idlewood."

"Historians!" Anna's mom hissed. "That makes sense."

"Of course we're trying to save it!" Emily's dad said. "It's a one-of-a-kind place with a rich history."

"Not rich enough!" Mr. Llewellyn said. He coughed and straightened his tie. "Idlewood is special, I won't disagree. My family wouldn't have acquired it if we didn't think so. Unfortunately, times change. An old house, odd as it is, isn't enough to drive tourists to the Virginian mountains anymore. And Idlewood requires so much maintenance."

Emily looked at him, understanding. "You can't afford to keep it. But you want to."

Mr. Llewellyn nodded. "If I could keep it, I would. I love this old house, and I haven't owned it for very long. My dream was to restore it to its glorious hotel days, and I tried, I really did. I cleaned the first floor and started to fix up the second, but then I learned we didn't have enough money to do a complete renovation of Idlewood. Or even to keep it. I found a buyer interested in the land, and I tried to convince them to keep the house the same, but I couldn't. The best I could do was give Idlewood a good send-off. Which is why I didn't want you," he said, facing Emily, "to blab about the sale. Let the people have a good time before it's gone."

"That's why we are here," Emily's mother said. "We thought we could have Idlewood named a historic location."

Mr. Llewellyn raised his hands. "Don't you think I tried that? The Gardners were rich but apparently not rich enough to be remembered. Yes, it has stayed the same, but that doesn't make it stand out enough. When I heard you wanted to come, I made sure you had a room here. I thought that if anyone could save Idlewood, it was the Shaughnessy historians. But I suppose you came too late."

"We'll see if you think that after you see this," Emily's dad said, raising the closed ledger.

Mr. Llewellyn leaned over it. "What is it?" Then his gray eyes bulged and he grabbed the edge of the book. "Where did you find this?"

Book Lady had peeked out of her room, a book (*Vandal and Visigoth*) under her arm, Suitcase Man right beside her. Emily tapped her dad's arm. "Maybe we should all go inside?"

"Yes, I think that's a good idea," Mr. Llewellyn said. He ushered Emily and her parents into the Rome suite, and glared at the Henderson kids, especially Anna, with her very dusty hair. "Don't you have somewhere to be?"

"Inside, with you," Anna said.

"We're part of this," Charlie added. He and Anna stepped past the gray man and into the Rome rooms. Their parents followed.

"We want to hear this story, too," Mr. Henderson said.

Once they were inside, Emily and Charlie sat on the purple couch. Anna stood next to them, finger-combing dust clumps out of her hair. The parents stood as well.

Mr. Llewellyn sat in a red armchair, the ledger spread on his knees. "Where did you find this?" he asked. "*How* did you find it? I've lived in this house for years, and I've never seen anything like it."

"We didn't," Emily's dad said. "It was actually Emily who brought it to us."

Mr. Llewellyn turned his gaze on the kids. "How did you—" He stopped, taking in the dust on their clothes and hair. "You were poking around, weren't you?"

Anna nodded. "I know you told me to stop, but we had to keep going. Did you know this house has a third floor?"

"I'd seen the windows, but I thought the third floor had been condemned," Mr. Llewellyn said. His voice was soft, distant. He glanced back at the ledger and then at the kids. "There was no staircase up from the second floor, you see. Why would it be sealed off if it wasn't dangerous? I hoped to fix it up someday, but with the financial worries and the impending loss of Idlewood, there didn't seem to be a point. I figured everything important had been moved to the main floors."

"You missed a couple of things," Anna said.

She launched into her part of the story, and Emily, and the others, listened with interest. This was the first time she'd heard Anna fully explain how she realized the house had a third floor, how she found the bookcase door and then the climbing entrances, and how she'd discovered Virginia Maines's tower room.

Taking the journal from Emily, Anna held it up.

"This has all kinds of stories written by Ginny, ones no one knows. And there are letters from her sister Elaine stored up there. The *real* Virginia Maines is up there, not the one that history remembers."

"So you found the ledger up there?" Mr. Llewellyn asked.

"Not exactly," Anna said. "We wouldn't have found it if it wasn't for Emily and Charlie breaking the code."

"A code," Emily cut in, "hidden in Idlewood's paintings and walls. Elaine left it there. That's why she ordered the house to remain unchanged."

"That's not the only reason," Charlie added. "Have you ever heard of Virginia's lost treasures?" When Mr. Llewellyn nodded, he said, "They're *here*. All of them." Charlie pointed at the Athena statue. "That's one of them."

"How do you know?" Mr. Llewellyn said.

Anna held out Virginia's journal. "Look," she said, turning to the photograph of the statue. "See? It's the same one. You can tell because they have the same cut on the shoulder."

Mr. Llewellyn jumped to his feet to examine the statue. "Are you sure? Are you *really* sure?"

"We are," Charlie said. "It's all in the journal. The penguin in the Arctic Circle suite was a friend of hers, and she brought him home with her after he died."

Emily nodded. "The house is probably full of them. These are Virginia's treasures, not gold and diamonds."

Mr. Llewellyn took the journal and carefully turned

a couple of pages. "How did you find all this after so many years?"

Together, Emily and Charlie told all about how Emily noticed that the paintings were different, which led her to the numbers in the China suite. And Charlie described how the odd, faded numbers on the doors were a cipher, which took him to the Rome suite. He stood and pointed out the code on the wall.

They told Mr. Llewellyn and their parents how the clues added up to a book cipher, and then Anna joined them when they talked about going to find a copy of *Treasure Island.*

"Because Anna read the journal, we knew the 'door between the dragon's wings' meant Virginia's airplane," Emily said. "So we went there and found a real door disguised as a fake one. Charlie figured out how to open it. There was a secret passage, leading to a small room. The ledger was hidden in there. Charlie figured out that the treasures were souvenirs Virginia brought back from her travels, and that Elaine was keeping them safe for her sister by ordering that the house remain unchanged."

"We can show you the passage to the secret room," Charlie said.

Anna nodded. "And the bookcase door," she said. "Though it might be locked."

Mr. Llewellyn closed the journal and handed it to Emily's dad. He stood up. "Take me there."

Grinning, Anna beckoned them after her as she went

out to the hall. Mr. Llewellyn followed, looking not quite as gray as usual.

Behind them went Charlie and Emily and all of their parents. "All this time, there was a puzzle in Idlewood?" her mother asked.

"How did no one see it?" her father responded.

Emily smiled. Maybe they had seen it. Or seen part of it, like Charlie and Anna and she all had. But without adding Anna's knowledge of Virginia's life to Emily's understanding of the way Idlewood used to be to Charlie's love of codes and puzzles, they would never have found the door.

Anna and Mr. Llewellyn stopped in the airplane room, where the hidden door still hung open. He touched the open door and peeked inside, down the dark hallway.

"The room's at the end," Anna said. "But it gets really dark in there."

Mr. Llewellyn pushed the door open wider. "All this time, this was here. And the ledger was at the end?"

"Yes," Emily said. "Though nothing else."

Mr. Llewellyn nodded and backed away. "Show me the bookcase door."

"It might not open," Anna warned.

"We'll see what we can do."

The group followed Anna to the bookcase. There, she and Emily looked at each other, took a deep breath, and pulled on the side of the shelf.

The door turned easily. Anna's jaw dropped. "What the? How?"

Emily patted her shoulder. "I guess we couldn't expect to solve *all* of Idlewood's mysteries in one weekend."

Mr. Llewellyn, with the air of someone entering a cathedral, went upstairs. Anna moved to follow him, but her mom grabbed her arm. "How did you find this place?"

"Poking around," Anna said. "I'm sorry. I know I wasn't supposed to. I've let you down, again."

"Oh, Anna." Mrs. Henderson shook her head, but she put an arm around her daughter. "We worry for your safety when you do things like this, and you need to learn how to explore the *right* way. But . . . at the same time, what you've done is incredible. I want you to be smart, and safe, and aware of what others don't want you doing, but I wouldn't trade you for anyone."

"Either of you," Mr. Henderson said, resting his hand on Charlie's shoulder. "Our daughter found out her hero lived here, and our son found a hidden code. Lucky us, to have such amazing kids!"

Emily watched as Anna turned as red as her hair. Without a word, the girl launched herself at her parents, hugging both of them. "Thank you," she said.

Emily's mother touched her daughter's arm. "They're not the only ones proud of their kid." She smiled at Emily.

I did it. Not on her own, but using her own methods, Emily had found the ledger. She'd found Virginia Maines at Idlewood and saved the house. She'd made her parents proud.

Emily followed Mr. Llewellyn up the stairs. He was

standing at the top, looking at the hall in front of him. Then he walked into the first room, one of the empty ones.

Emily found him at the closet, touching a faded blue dress. "These were the rooms they lived in," he said. "All this time, it was here."

"At the end of the hall is the door to the tower room," Emily said. "All of Virginia's things are still there. Her maps, her books. Everything."

Mr. Llewellyn didn't answer. Emily stepped closer. "Well?" she asked. "Do you think this will be enough to make this place a historic location? Can you save Idlewood?"

The owner of the house turned around. His eyes glistened. "Yes, Emily. I think we have all we need."

19

MR. LLEWELLYN holed up in his office, calling anyone he could reach in the company that was going to buy Idlewood and planning a formal request for the Virginia Historical Society, with Emily and her parents hanging around outside. Last time Charlie had seen Emily, she was sitting in the entry hall, the ledger and letter in her lap. She was grinning like a National Spelling Bee winner. As Charlie had passed, she'd waved at him.

He'd waved back, heading out to the grounds. His parents had made him and Anna retell the whole story. Charlie and Anna had left some parts out, like climbing the wall to the tower, although when they'd reached that part, Anna had nudged Charlie slightly and smiled at him. He'd smiled back.

The other guests had no idea what had happened. Rosie and Xavier had already been arrested after being revealed as thieves. The thieving Haskells were also gone, as Charlie had proved by a thorough search of the grounds. Anna wondered if they'd already realized that the treasure they took was nothing more than party props, or if they still thought they'd struck it rich.

But the young family with the matching T-shirts (which now said WAVE AT THE OCEAN—they must have run out of Idlewood-themed shirts) and the honeymooners and the tour group and all the rest were still stinging from being suspected of theft, and once the search was over, many of them retired to their rooms or hurried outside.

Charlie thought they had the right idea and went out to the grounds. He took a deep breath of the humid air. As comfortable as it was in a quiet corner of the library, reading a book, sometimes it was better to go outside and breathe in the big, wide world.

Virginia Maines must have felt the same way. How many mountain ranges did she breathe in? And, he wondered, walking to the evergreen maze, where had she breathed in her last? Had she been murdered by Everett, like Anna suggested, or had she fled the charges against her? If she ran, where did she go?

"Hey! Wait for me!"

Charlie turned to see Anna barreling toward him. Slowing, she ran past him and circled back. "Hey," she said. "Wild morning, huh?"

Her hair was still gray with dust in some places. With its red dimmed, Charlie thought he could see a resemblance between his sister and Virginia. Both of them had the same satisfied grin. He could almost imagine Anna pulling an ancient relic out of her pocket and winking.

She had Virginia's journal in her hand. That added to the image.

"No kidding," he said. "I really needed to get away from all the noise for a while."

"Me too." She looked at the maze. "This looks like a good place to go missing," she said. "I haven't explored it yet."

"I know the way to the center," Charlie said. "I can show you."

Anna shook her head. "It's better if we just wander."

She walked into the maze, and Charlie joined her. They traveled in silence for a while. Here in the middle of the bushes, Charlie could hear the hubbub of some of the other guests, but it was muted under the sound of wind in the trees and birdsong. Not to mention his own thoughts.

"There's so much more we still don't know!" he blurted out to Anna.

"I know!" she said. "We still have no idea how Ginny just vanished. I thought, with all those clues, we'd learn *something.*"

"Or why there was that *Treasure Island* cover in the box. It couldn't be a clue to our code—it came way too late. If we got that far, then of course we already knew we needed the book!"

"And I found this key." She pulled out the tarnished key. "But I never found a lock. Where does it belong?"

"And did Virginia ever come back?" Charlie added. "Did she ever get Elaine's message?"

"I don't know. I hope so." Anna shook her head. "The more I learn about this house, the less sense it makes. Like, I understand now, knowing that Ginny and Elaine lived here, why there's such a big library and why there's an exotic plant garden, and even the themed rooms make sense. Ginny was an explorer, and her sister wanted to honor that."

They'd somehow wandered back to the mouth of the maze. Emily was standing outside, hand shading her eyes as she peered over the grounds. When she spotted the Hendersons, she grinned and ran over. "Hey, you missed it!" she said. "Mr. Llewellyn just told my parents that he's canceled his plans to sell Idlewood. He's going to announce to the world our findings about Virginia Maines. Before long, this place will be full of historians and then tourists. We saved Idlewood!" She pulled them both into a group hug.

"That's great, Emily," Charlie said. "And the treasures?"

"Well, I thought since Anna stole the journal—"

"I didn't *steal* anything. You can have it back if you want," Anna said, holding it out.

Emily waved it away. "I was thinking that it would be a big help to Mr. Llewellyn if we got a list together of as many treasures as we could identify. Down for another treasure hunt?"

"Sure!" It wasn't the same as the hunt they'd just had, but hey, Charlie loved any kind of puzzle. And he was curious to find what Elaine had put in each room to honor Virginia.

"Me too," Anna said as they followed Emily into the house.

"There's the statue in Rome, and the penguin," Emily said. "Any others we know about?"

"An ink painting from China," Anna said, grinning.

The three spent the rest of the day hunting. The adults had finally been briefed on the events of the day, so they seemed happy to let the kids search for the great explorer's hidden treasures.

The elderly women oohed and aahed over the pair of alabaster sphinxes left in the Egypt suite.

A set of carved wooden animals in the Serengeti suite pleased the Sunglasses Couple, but only after the woman chatted with the kids in the sitting room for several minutes before the husband showed up and told them they could look in every room but the bathroom, which needed to stay closed.

Macaw feathers in the Amazon room, and Book Lady had been using one as a bookmark.

A tartan cloth draped on a wall in the ballroom.

On, and on, and on, until everything Virginia had named in her journal had been found. And with each treasure came a story. The carved animals were actually Virginia's own handiwork—a man in Hwange had taught her. The macaw feathers came from a bird eaten in the deep jungle when all hope seemed lost for rescue—and then, it came the next day. The tartan was a replica of an ancient, damaged cloth Virginia had found in a hidden room in a Scotland castle and wanted to preserve in some way.

Eventually, they ran out of places to search and went back to the grounds to rest in the grass.

The girls were talking quietly, sharing the journal and its stories. Charlie, on the other hand, was looking up at the tower. He thought of Virginia up there, examining new treasures and remembering the people she'd met, the places she'd learned about, and smiling.

Did she ever get scared out there, alone? Was that why she felt such a connection with the people in the lands she visited? With her treasures all around her, did she feel like, in some way, those people had come home with her?

"Hey, anyone want to see if we can have dinner outside tonight?" Charlie asked.

The girls looked up. Emily shrugged. "I guess. It would be a nice way to end the trip. Let's go see if we can grab a picnic basket or something."

Anna stood up. "I know a great rock we can sit on," she said, grinning at Charlie.

Charlie sighed and followed them back into the house. Maybe he shouldn't have suggested a picnic. If Anna got her way, he'd have to climb back up that big rock in the woods.

Then again, Charlie thought, looking back up at the tower, if he did, that was going to be one more amazing thing he did while at Idlewood. Maybe he could bring a pebble back with him, to remember it by.

20

IT WAS MONDAY, and Anna felt like she was leaving home. She never thought she'd care so much about Idlewood, but before Friday, she never knew that Virginia Maines had also once called this place home.

She and Charlie and Emily had gotten permission to pack a picnic dinner the night before and take it out to the grounds. If the rock was slightly off the grounds, no one seemed to care. Charlie had climbed up all by himself, no guidance needed, though Anna had noticed he was gritting his teeth the whole way up.

They had eaten their sandwiches and talked about Idlewood and the mystery they'd solved until it got dark. Emily told stories about the house in its heyday, and Anna read entries from Ginny's journal, as they would soon have to release it to Mr. Llewellyn and the Shaughnessys. They played games and exchanged contact information, and considered sleeping out there under the stars (Charlie's idea, believe it or not) before that was quickly shot down by the Henderson parents when they came to retrieve their offspring.

Anna had found it hard to sleep back in her room, under the calligraphy painting that was one of Ginny's treasures (though, now, perhaps all the guests felt that way). Idlewood had been the world for one weekend, and now it was time to leave that world and return to the real one. Anna had a feeling that somehow nothing would be the same ever again, that this small world could change the larger one.

As the Hendersons ate breakfast, Anna and Charlie spent the meal chatting about the house and plans for next weekend. Charlie thought he could come up with a code more elaborate than Elaine Gardner's, and he wanted Anna to try to solve it. He promised it would be worth her time but wouldn't say anything else.

"You're smart," he'd said. "I'll have to make it really challenging." Which made Anna smile.

Anna, on the other hand, had some forest trails she thought Charlie would like. One led to an old millhouse. Not really Idlewood, but at least there would be no climbing. Charlie should like that.

After breakfast it was checkout time. Anna packed up her things quickly, and while her parents took their sweet time loading their toothbrushes back into the toiletry bags, and Charlie went to visit Emily before the Shaughnessys left (Emily's parents were planning to write another book, this time about Virginia Maines and

Idlewood), Anna snuck up through the bookcase door to say goodbye to Ginny.

"You know, we never did figure out why this door locked itself sometimes," she muttered as she went up to the dusty third floor.

There were so many things they hadn't figured out. Sure, they cleared Ginny's name. Sure, Charlie found the treasure, scattered throughout Idlewood.

But as Anna climbed into the tower room, she bristled over the loose ends. "What are you for?" she asked, pulling the black key out of her pocket and running her thumb over its palm tree design. "What happened to Virginia?"

Had Everett Gardner killed her to protect his secret? Anna doubted it. Virginia Maines was a legend. Some rich guy who couldn't win against a mountain lion wouldn't be able to take her out when a pride of actual lions couldn't.

No. Faced with false accusation, with the threat of being locked away from the big, beautiful world she loved, Ginny had fled. Anna was sure of it. It was what she would have done. It was what Anna *had* done when accused of theft.

The tower room was still and silent. Sunlight streamed through the dingy window, illuminating the scattered charts, clothes, and books. But now, dust had been wiped from the desk. Footprints had turned the floor into the map of an energetic dance.

And on the bed was the coverless copy of *Treasure*

Island, right where Charlie had left it before climbing down the tower.

Anna carried the book back over to the desk and sat down. She set the black key on the desk. It didn't belong to her, after all. Even though she'd found it in the woods, it seemed like it belonged here, with all the other mysteries. Then she opened the book and idly turned the pages. For now, she just wanted to bask in the tower room and the feeling of history that hung around here.

Down below, the guests were leaving. The tour group had already gone. The Shaughnessys were talking with Mr. Llewellyn. Suitcase Man and Book Lady approached each other, then closed in a passionate kiss that made Anna blush and look away, to where the Sunglasses Couple carried a bundle back to their car. As Anna watched, a little dog's head emerged from the cloth.

Anna laughed. That explained a lot. The howl Charlie had heard! The off-limits bathroom! And those "cookies" the T-shirt kids kept going after must have been dog biscuits.

The sea of trees outside the window danced in the breeze. Huh. She never had gotten around to checking out that other building. The wooden roof really *did* look like a raft out there. Like Ginny's raft.

Anna frowned and stared out the window, a brittle page between two fingers. Why had Elaine left the cover of this book down there with the ledger? Her frown deepened into a scowl as she turned pages absentmindedly. It was like the third-floor windows; Anna could feel an answer waiting, but she couldn't reach it! Emily might have been right with her "some mysteries aren't meant to be solved" spiel, but Anna didn't want to accept it. There was too much that didn't add up, like the way the Rome suite used a Caesar cipher, the same kind of code Elaine praised in her letters to Ginny, and the code word of the Caesar cipher was *dragon*, Ginny's childhood nickname, and the portrait changes would only stick out to someone who knew the house before it was altered. It was almost like the whole code was *meant* for one person, and that person was—

Anna froze, looking at the book in front of her. *Treasure Island*. They'd found its cover, with its childish scribble of a tree house, hidden with the ledger.

She sat, thinking, and then searched through the letters until she found the one she was looking for. "Perhaps one day," Elaine had written, "we will build one, just you and me, and we can model it after the one you, in your frustration, drew on the cover of *Treasure Island*, just so the book would have at least one tree house!"

It *had* to be the same book cover, and the same doodle. Ginny had drawn that picture because she'd been so upset that the story didn't have . . . "No way," Anna breathed.

She looked up through the window, her eyes resting on the wooden roof. The roof of a building so high up that no one could see it except from a tower window.

Standing up so fast her chair wobbled, Anna grabbed the key and bolted down the tower, through the third floor, and back into the main Idlewood house. All the while, her mind played the events of the past like a movie.

Elaine finds the real ledger and realizes her sister is innocent, but it's too late and Ginny has already vanished. Feeling guilty and wanting to make amends but unable to keep Idlewood, Elaine oversees the renovation of the house into a hotel, turning it not only into a friendly lodge for travelers but also a nest of clues that would be recognized by someone who knows Idlewood, someone who understands codes, and someone who loves exploration as much as she loves her family. Just in case she came back before Elaine got a chance to return to Idlewood herself.

At the end of that line of clues? An apology. The truth. One sister telling another that she loved her, to please come home.

But had Virginia ever returned to Idlewood? Ever seen Elaine's message?

Racing across the grounds, Anna had her own ideas on the subject. Elaine hadn't left the cover of *Treasure Island* in that box. She had no reason to. But someone else did.

"Anna!" Charlie was calling, his backpack in his hand. Emily was standing beside him. "Where have you been? Mom and Dad are packing up the car. We're about to leave."

"Charlie. I—I just need a few minutes. Stall them, please? There's something I need to do. Alone."

Charlie and Emily looked from her flushed face to

the key in her hand. Anna could practically see their mental math calculating, determining that *she has found something.*

He nodded. "Do what you have to do."

"But tell us everything!" Emily added.

Anna smiled and raced off into the forest, not stopping until, breathless, she came to a halt beneath a big tree. A tree that used to have an old key buried beneath it.

This was a rainy area. Water and mud could have carried the key downhill, wedged it up against another tree's root, and covered it with debris. If Anna turned and walked uphill, she might find—

Another tree, older than the first. Boards were nailed to it, making a ladder to the top. And up above, she knew a tree house waited.

A tree house that, even in a world of GPS and satellite images, had been missed, kept secret, saved. Its key, lost. Until Anna had found it.

The boards were old, probably rotten. But Anna didn't let that stop her. She tested the first board, and when it held her weight, she moved to the next. A few of the boards had worn down to little more than sticks, but they worked fine until Anna was high enough to use branches instead.

Soon, she was at the top. A small porch jutted out from a square shack, and Anna pulled herself up to it. A door with a silver lock, tarnished black, barred her way.

Anna slid the black key she'd found a whole weekend

ago, with its palm tree design, into the lock. It fit beautifully, and after a little work, the door clicked open.

She stepped inside, leaving the key behind in the lock. A bare wooden room met her—no shelves, no furniture except for one wooden table in front of a window. It looked just like the hidden room where the ledger had been stored.

Anna laughed. "Nice one." She dropped to the floor and slid under the table, just as she had in the hidden room. The floor smelled like mildew and pine sap.

And under the table, fastened to the underside, was a small, cloth-wrapped package. Anna pried it free and crawled out. Fingers trembling, she undid the cloth.

Inside was a metal picture frame, nothing else. But the black-and-white picture was of a family: husband, wife, two kids. They stood on a dock somewhere with palm trees, a boat behind them.

The man, fair-haired, held the younger child in one arm. The other arm was wrapped around his wife's waist. She was laughing, holding on to the older child's shoulder with one hand and resting the other on a pile of crates. Her dark, curly hair flew in the wind. A dragon-shaped brooch was fastened near her throat.

"Hello, Ginny," Anna said, touching the picture. She smiled at Virginia, and then at the child the great explorer was touching. The girl had inherited her father's light hair but also Ginny's curls.

Anna carefully pulled the picture out of the frame. Turning it over, she read, "The Taylor family."

After all the years and questions, here was the answer. Ginny had left, chased away from Idlewood by false accusations. And she'd come back, hoping to find her sister, but instead just found the clues Elaine had left for her.

And the tree house? Elaine had loved Idlewood and Virginia knew that. Virginia must have known that sooner or later, her sister would come back, perhaps to stay in Idlewood again, but if not, at least to check on her own code, and would have the chance to find the tree house, the one thing Virginia had wanted but never got. So she built it herself, and left her own clues in the form of the book cover and the key so Elaine would recognize the tree house for what it was and be able to enter it as she wanted to.

It had been so long.

Had Elaine ever found this tree house before she died? How did that key end up buried beneath a tree? Had Virginia carelessly left it on the tree-house porch, where rain and wind could knock it free, sending it tumbling into the mud? Or had another hand brought the key here, carried it from a hidden box where it rested beside an old, scribbled-on book cover? Could Elaine have come back to check on her message and found a response that told her that Ginny was alive and well?

Anna knew what *she* believed had happened. After all, Ginny was many things, but careless was not one of them.

"Anna! Where are you?"

Anna started. Her family.

She slid the photo back into the frame and set the picture up on the table. Then she left, locking the door behind her.

Anna climbed down and returned to her family on Idlewood's grounds. She smiled at them and said, "Just saying goodbye to the forest" before following them back to their car.

Emily was there waiting, and she and Charlie pulled Anna aside.

"What did you find?" Charlie asked.

"Tell you later," she whispered to them. Her parents were too close. "Emily, watch for my email."

Later, she would tell them what she'd found. But only Charlie and Emily. Ginny had kept her secret all her life, so Anna would keep it, too.

But she had left the black key on the porch, right next to the tree-house door, because maybe someday, another explorer could follow the clues preserved in Idlewood, the codes and messages, and find this tree house before the Shenandoah forests reclaimed it. That person might climb the ladder to the tree house, searching it out for no other reason than to *know*. To find a place untouched, unexplored. They might one day find the picture and learn the truth of what happened to Ginny Maines. And if they came, they'd need the key.

As the Hendersons drove away, Anna rolled down the window and looked back. Idlewood glowed in the morning sun like a golden temple, and the wind tousled Anna's curls like an ocean breeze.

She blew a kiss at Idlewood and sank back into the car. There were still questions and mysteries left to solve, hidden areas to explore, and Anna itched to find every answer, every cranny. She would reach horizons over mountains, seas, deserts, maybe even outer space! She'd find her place among those who needed to know what lay beyond.

As Idlewood shrank into its cover of forest, having given up its counsel to a bunch of kids, the "normal" world would be an adventure of its own. Anna couldn't wait to get started.

THE EXPLORER'S CODES (AND PUZZLES)

Hello, reader!

This book uses a variety of codes and puzzles, like the Atbash cipher, the keyed Caesar, and the book code. Although, in this story, the codes are used by fictional characters, they are all very real and have been used for centuries by people wanting to keep their messages secret.

You can try it yourself! Try using one of the codes in this book to write a secret message to a family member or a friend. It's a fun way to share a secret, or just say "hello" with a different flair. SZEV UFM! (Atbash for "Have fun!")

ACKNOWLEDGMENTS

Writing a book requires a team of people with wonderful, different skills to make it happen. So, I would be a rude and ungrateful writer if I didn't thank the people who helped this story go from being a dream to a reality. Thank you, Lauren E. Abramo, my agent and friend, who encouraged me to continue writing this story and for helping me find the best place to send it.

And on that note, thanks also goes to John Morgan, my editor at Imprint, for believing in the story and for being such a fun, friendly editor to work with as we polished *The Explorer's Code* for final publication. I've enjoyed it.

I'd also like to thank Imprint's publisher, Erin Stein, creative director Natalie C. Sousa, managing editor Dawn Ryan, and production manager Raymond Ernesto Colón, as well as Carolyn Bull for my cover. Making a book is such a team effort, and I have a great team.

Thanks to my writing group who read this story and gave me my first round of revisions to complete. You make me better, and I hope to one day be half the writers you all already are.

I also want to thank my family, of course. Thank you, Mom and Dad, for always supporting me (and not questioning how I spent my holiday mornings outlining this book). Thank you, Grace, Brian, Chrisanne, and David, my amazing siblings. And, of course, many thanks to Spencer, my best friend and husband, who has never been anything but loving and supportive.

About the Author

ALLISON K. HYMAS was born on the anniversary of the day Amelia Earhart became the first woman to fly nonstop and solo across the Atlantic. She was born in Utah and raised in Virginia and Pennsylvania, where she enjoyed spending time in the mountains and forests. Allison is also the author of *Under Locker and Key* and *Arts and Thefts*. She currently lives in Provo, Utah, where she teaches writing, visits national parks, and runs very long distances for fun.